ARRANGED

CARFANO CRIME FAMILY
BOOK 7

REBECCA GANNON

Copyright © 2025 Rebecca Gannon
All rights reserved.

ISBN: 9798306394183

No part of this book may be reproduced or transmitted in any means, electronic or mechanical, including photocopying, recording, or by any information storage and retrieval system without the written permission of the author, except for the use of brief quotations in a review.

This book is a work of fiction. Names, characters, places, and incidents are either products of the author's imagination or are used fictitiously. Any resemblance to actual persons, living or dead, events, or locales is entirely coincidental.

newsletter, contact me, blog, shop, and links to all social medias:
www.rebeccagannon.com

Content Warning

This book contains course language, violence, and explicit adult content that's intended for readers 18 and older, with a warning that this is an arranged/forced marriage mafia book. With that, comes situations and scenarios that may make some readers uncomfortable.

More by Rebecca Gannon

Pine Cove
Her Maine Attraction
Her Maine Reaction
Her Maine Risk
Her Maine Distraction

Carfano Crime Family
Casino King
The Boss
Vengeance
Executioner
Wild Ace
Captivated
Arranged

Standalone Novels
Whiskey & Wine
Redeeming His Reputation

To everyone who wishes a mysterious dark and handsome man would come along and tell you he's obsessed with you, has secretly been watching you, and you must marry him or else…
This book is for you.

THE CARFANO FAMILY

Leo (d)
(m) Katarina (d)
|

Michael (d)	Salvatore (d)	Anthony	Richard	Maria
(m) Anita	(m) Teresa	(m) Francesca	(m) Christina	(m) Carmine
|	|	|	|	|
Leo, Alec,	Nico, Vincenzo,	Stefano, Marco,	Saverio,	Matteo, Elena
Luca, Katarina	Mia	Gabriel	Gia, Aria	

(m) – married / (d) – deceased

She's not mine yet
I don't think you can belong to someone
Anymore
But how I would love her
If she could be mine

- Courtney Peppernell

"Pillow Thoughts III:
Mending the Mind"

CHAPTER 1
Santino

I tap my fingers on the leather beside my thigh and rub my chin, preparing myself for what I'm about to walk into.

Leo Carfano called a meeting with me, and as the head of the Carfano family, the most powerful of the four remaining families, he's someone who leaves no room for any response other than yes.

The last time I made the drive to the Carfano building, I was with my father. I was the only one of the two of us to make it out of there alive, and for good reason. My father shouldn't have gone against Leo. It got him a bullet in the brain from their enforcer.

We were supposed to merge the Carfano and Antonucci families last year with a marriage between myself and Leo's sister, Katarina, but that didn't happen. And it was never going to happen so long as the Carfano's enforcer had anything to say about it. Dante Salerno is not a man I'd ever cross or be the one that stands between him and his girl. He probably contemplated killing me every which way to Sunday from the moment he thought I was going to be the man Katarina was going to marry.

After my father was killed, my grandfather officially stepped down as the head of the family, passing that title to me. Since I've taken over, the Carfanos and Antonuccis have been civil, with no bad blood harbored between us.

"You can wait out here," I tell my driver, Vince, when we pull up outside the Carfano building.

"Are you sure, Boss?"

"Yes, I'll be fine." He nods, and I climb out of the back of the town car, looking up at the black building that holds not just my future, but my family's.

I'm prepared for the same deal as last time.

I'm prepared to marry the girl I can't close my damn eyes without seeing.

I'm let through at security with a simple nod and directed towards the elevators where another guard swipes a card to allow me access. He punches in a code and scans his fingerprint before hitting the button for the third floor and stepping back into the lobby like a robot.

Jesus, his job must be mind-numbingly boring.

The doors close and I stare at my stony reflection in the shiny metal, keeping my mask I shuttered into place the moment I stepped out of the car. I know they know I'm here. I know they can see me in their security footage, and I refuse to show any emotion that they could misread into thinking I'm a weak pissant who will do whatever they want or say without negotiation.

I know they're in trouble. I've heard the rumblings about the sabotage to their trucks over the last couple months, and I know they're at the point of needing me if they called a meeting.

I hold the cards.

I have something they need, and if they want me to help them, then they're going to give me what I want in return.

Who I want in return.

The elevator doors slide open and I take long strides towards the conference room occupied by a table of Carfanos. I'm sure it's meant to intimidate me, and if we were meeting in the basement like last time, I might be, but here in their glass castle, I find I'm not intimidated in the least. They may hold more power than me, but I know they need me, which gives me all the power I need to push open the glass door and step into the room like I own the fucking place. Like I'm one of them.

"Santino," Leo greets, standing to shake my hand.

"Leo," I reply in the same curt tone, gripping his hand firmly.

"Thanks for meeting us today."

"Of course." I nod, then give a nod to the other men sitting around the table.

Luca is Leo's brother and underboss. Nico is Leo's cousin and right-hand-man. Basically, his second underboss. Vinny is Nico's brother, who runs Atlantic City and their casino, The Aces, along with Leo's other brother, Alec, who is absent today. Then there's Stefano, Marco, and Gabriel. They're Leo's cousins and the family's main *capos* in their ranks. Stefano is also the best hacker in the city, if not the entire eastern seaboard. His talents are well-known amongst all the organizations in the city.

"Have a seat." Leo gestures to the chair opposite his at the other end of the table. The chairs on either side of me are empty while they sit as a united front before me. It's a glaring message as to how they view me. I'm opposite them. I'm separate from them.

Well, not for fucking long if I get what I want.

Seven pairs of eyes are on me, but I wait for Leo to speak first. "I asked you here because I wanted to discuss a business deal with you."

"You need my trucks," I state flatly, and his eyes don't give away a single emotion or ounce of surprise that I already know this. "How many have you lost now?"

"Enough that we're having this meeting."

"Someone is trying to ruin you and your reputation. Do you know who?"

"Yes, and I know you're not involved," he tells me, as if that's supposed to assuage me. I never knew he suspected me, but I should have.

My father went against Leo when he was contacted by the crazy fucking Albanian mafia leader of the Aleksanyan family. He stupidly agreed to give him the when and where of a meeting we were having with the Carfanos as a get-to-know-you lunch with Katarina.

That shit ended with bullets flying into the restaurant after my father and I left, and then a bullet in my dad's brain when it was discovered he was the rat.

I swallow my feelings on that matter to remain focused on the here and now. My dad was an asshole and he didn't think it through when he went against Leo. Hovan was a crazy motherfucker, but all my dad had to do was tell Leo what was up, and we could have smoked him out and taken him out. Together.

I hate my father for that. I hate him for a lot of reasons, but that's the one that's still touching me from his grave.

If I didn't stand up and pledge my innocence to Leo and assure him of my ignorance to my dad's plan, I would've been killed right alongside him. It was the truth, too. I didn't know about what my dad did and I never would've agreed to it if he had brought it up to me.

If Hovan chose to come for us, we'd have had the help of the Carfanos. But of course, my dad was blind to the notion that all the top Carfanos would be taken out in one go rather than seeing the whole picture. He was always consumed with the need to be on their level rather than handling our business and growing our portfolios.

He was a power-hungry bastard.

Working with the Carfanos would have achieved us a new level of power, but of course, that wouldn't have been good enough for my father. Leo would have gladly worked with us to take that fucker out. Hell, he already wiped out the rest of his goddamn family, which is why Hovan was so hell-bent on destroying the Carfanos and anyone else who got in his way.

"I have no reason to want you or your family gone," I tell Leo. "If you are, then my family, and the others, are all fucked. Every foreign and domestic organization will move in and fight us for what you'd leave behind."

Leo gives me a curt nod. "We recently found out that it's some cousin of Hovan and Diran that's seeking revenge. He appears to have more stealth than his cousins by the way he's been able to skirt our security and discover our routes, even though we alter them each time. He's been picking off our trucks one by one over the past few months, and just a couple days ago, he targeted and took out another two in the same fucking day. The trucks, their contents, and our drivers. All gone. Every time."

"You have a broken link in your chain."

Anger flashes in Leo's eyes while his face remains like stone. "I know. He was dealt with last night. But that doesn't mean I don't still have a problem that you can help me with."

"You need my trucks."

"Yes. Your business is doing well, but if you merge with us, then you'll be flushed with fucking cash."

The Antonuccis have operated a fleet of refrigerated food,

beverage, and liquor trucks that make deliveries all over the tri-state area. Five years ago, though, my father expanded the business and aligned with the fucking Gulf Cartel to transport their drugs from shipping containers at Red Hook Terminal in Brooklyn disguised inside crates of coffee, to warehouses in the Bronx, Newark, Philly, and New Haven, where they cut and package it for distribution.

I never would have made that deal, but once again, my father was a greedy bastard that wanted to have as much power as the men sitting before me.

"I have conditions," I tell Leo.

"I thought as much."

"I want out of the deal my father made with the Gulf Cartel five years ago. We pick up their product from the port, then transport it to four cities. I don't trust them and I hate dealing with them. You can have those trucks if you can help me sever ties."

Leo is quiet for a minute, and it's Luca who clears his throat before speaking. "We can give the business to the Melccionas. I know they just got a blow from the Jamaicans who took over their smaller drug smuggling operation. They'd love a new in to the game and the cash flow."

"Alright, we'll schedule a meeting with them," Leo says, then cuts his eyes back to mine. "Done."

"Not quite."

Leo's jaw flexes at my words. "What else?" This is fucking killing him to not be the one who has what someone else needs for once.

"I want the same deal as last time."

"And what exactly was that?"

Is he playing dumb?

"I want a connection to your family so I know you won't screw me over and muscle me out once the ink dries on the contract. You wouldn't fuck me over if I was married to one of your women. It'd fuck you over right back, and who knows what I'd do if I were angry enough."

The tension in the room skyrockets in a matter of milliseconds at my declaration. "If that's how you view marriage and women, what makes you think I'd allow that?" Leo questions, his emotions finally cracking through his mask of steel.

"I never said that it was. I just stated what would happen if you chose to make a move to fuck me over and renege on our deal. I didn't say I'd want to or would enjoy doing it. It's just a promised consequence if it comes to that."

I keep eye contact with Leo, never wavering, and not letting him find a single doubt in my gaze.

"As you know, Katarina is taken now." Leo's eyes flick to Nico and Vinny, and I have to hold back from smirking like an asshole.

"I know."

His brows twitch. "It seems you have someone in mind."

"I want Mia."

I can feel the glares of Nico and Vinny, her brothers, but my deal is with Leo, not them, so I keep my eyes on him.

"You want Mia," he states, his eyes narrowing.

"Yes."

"Why her?"

"Why not her? I saw her at your wedding. She's beautiful."

When I saw Mia six months ago at Leo's wedding, I was fucking awe struck. She's fucking gorgeous. I spent the entire night watching her laugh, smile, and talk to her family. And when she got up to dance with her cousins, I had to hold back the urge to walk right up to her and wrap my arms around her waist and have her grind that sexy ass of hers against me.

She wasn't hiding any of her curves in that silk bridesmaid dress she had on. My cock was hard as fucking steel from the moment I saw her walk down the aisle to the time I got home to jerk off, picturing everything I wished I could do to her.

Everyone watched Leo and Abrianna get married, but I watched Mia Carfano. The way her hips swayed, the way she smiled when they said their vows, and the way she teared up when they kissed as husband and wife. She blinked away her tears before they could fall, and I could see the mix of joy and envy in her gaze as she followed them back down the aisle.

Mia never once noticed me that night, but I noticed everything about her. And since then, I've learned everything I could find out about her.

"She is." His jaw ticks. "I could arrange for you to meet her."

I can't help the slight upturn of my lips. "Perfect. But it's her or there's no deal."

Leo's jaw flexes again, no doubt in an attempt to not tell me to fuck off. Vinny, though, isn't as adept at keeping his emotions in check, because he grunts his opposition and I finally let my eyes flit over to his and Nico's. Leo is able to school is emotions for the most part, but these two are showing nothing but anger and flat-out contempt towards me.

I know I should care what they think because they're Mia's brothers, but I can't bring myself to at the moment. They can hate me all they want, but if they want this deal to happen, then I'm going to marry their sister and they're going to have to accept that.

"We'll talk to Mia and then we can all meet next Friday. And considering how the meeting of you and Katarina ended last year, you'll come here," he says forcefully, his pointer finger touching the table to punctuate *here*. "Same time."

"Sounds perfect to me." Standing, I make eye contact with each of the men around the table. "Until then." I nod, and take my leave, waiting until I'm out of sight before letting my smile spread across my face.

She'll soon be mine.

CHAPTER 2
Mia

"What are you saying?" I ask my brothers, my eyes darting between Nico and Vinny. I know what I'm hearing, but I'm hoping by some miracle I've lost my faculties and I've imagined they just told me I was going to be marrying Santino Antonucci.

"You're marrying Santino," Leo, my cousin and the head of the family, tells me instead of my brothers.

"Why? I know Katarina was supposed to last year, but I thought that was all resolved or whatever."

"What was resolved?"

"I don't know!" I say, throwing my hands in the air.

"Whatever the reason was that you needed her to marry him last year. Can't you just negotiate whatever business deal you need to make with him without marrying me off?"

"He wants you," Leo says through a tight jaw, like it was difficult to say.

I suck in a sharp breath. "What the hell does that mean? He wants me? He said *me* specifically?" I point to my chest.

"Yes." Nico scrubs his hands down his face, clearly not liking that he had to admit that.

My eyes widen. "Why?"

"He saw you at my wedding," Leo tells me, "and he wants you as part of the deal or there's no deal."

I really don't know how I should take that…

Flattered or weirded out?

He saw me six months ago and decided he wants me for life? Who the hell is this guy? He has to be certifiable. And why is he so desperate for a wife? Can't he find one on his own?

Wait, of course he can't, because then she wouldn't be a Carfano and wouldn't give him the power I'm assuming he's after by linking himself to my family.

"Why do I have to do this? You can't negotiate without me?"

"The family needs you to do this. *I* need you to do this," Leo emphasizes.

"Why?" I ask again. "You ask me here to tell me I'll be marrying a complete stranger because he decided he wants me, and I'm supposed to just accept that?"

I've been the 'good girl' my entire life. I've always done

what my parents asked of me, and after my father was killed, I did what my brothers asked of me. My family is everything to me, but this is fucking crazy. I thought it was crazy when they tried to pawn Katarina off on this guy, but I bit my tongue on the matter because it ended up working out as it was supposed to – with her and Dante together.

But now? Me? I'm supposed to fall on the sword for my family so they can get richer and control me even more?

"Yes, you are," Leo tells me, both of our frustrations growing the longer this is drawn out.

"That's not an answer, Leo."

"The family needs you, Mia," Nico says. "We're in trouble and need Santino's help. The only way he'll provide that help is if he's tied to our family so we won't think of screwing him over in the deal."

"And I'm that tie," I say quietly, finishing his thought.

"Yes."

"Why do you need his help? Aren't you Leo Carfano? You can't get what you need without him?"

Leo's jaw ticks, his frustrations hanging by a thread. "Someone is trying to bring us down, Mia," he finally admits. "We're being targeted, and we need you to step up and do this for the family. Don't think that me, or your brothers, wanted to ask this of you, but here we are. We need you. I can promise you that this isn't easy for me, and I can promise you that as a Carfano, you're the one who will hold all the power in the relationship."

Relationship.

"What kind of relationship will there be if it's one-sided and forced?"

"Whatever kind you tell him it will be. You're not forced to do anything with him, Mia. I'll make that fucking clear to him. He messes up, and he's dead. No questions. No explanations. No second chances. I promise you that. Fuck any deal we make if he tries any shit with you, okay?"

I swallow the lump of emotions crawling their way up my throat and look over at my brothers. I can see the mix of regret and need for me to agree in their eyes, pleading with me to understand and do this for them.

I've always done what was asked of me. I've always tried to remain in the background so I didn't rock the boat or get in the way of anyone. Growing up, I knew that my father was, and brothers are, important to the family. More so than myself. But now I'm needed, and as Leo said, it's on my terms. Which means I can make whatever rules I want in the marriage. I'll have to find a way to take control from the beginning, because I already know I have to do this for my family. I can't disappoint them. It's not in me to walk away and leave my loved ones in trouble. If I can help, I'm going to, and they know it.

Taking a deep breath, I straighten my spine and look each of them in the eyes before finally agreeing. "Fine."

Leo sits back in his chair and rubs his jaw. "Thank you, Mia."

"When will this happen?"

"Soon. You'll meet him Friday."

"Will it be in front of all of you?" I ask, not holding back my dismay.

"Yes, why?" he asks, as if I'm the odd one for asking that.

"Because it's awkward enough without having my family watch me be sold off as cattle."

"Jesus, Mia, that's not what's happening."

"It is. Even if you don't see it that way, that's exactly what's happening." Standing, I smooth my hands down the sides of my skirt and loop my purse into the crook of my arm before walking out of there with my head held high. I refuse to cry in front of them or throw a fit like a child.

I'll find a way to make this my own.

I'll find a way to gain control.

I'll find a way to have Santino Antonucci wishing he never chose me as his bargaining chip. He doesn't know me. And hell, if I annoy or piss him off enough, maybe he'll ask me for a divorce within a few months. Problem solved.

CHAPTER 3
Mia

"Are you home this week? Are you going out tonight? Because I need you to take me to the best club you know so I can dress up and dance," I say to my cousin, Aria, as soon as she answers the phone. Her and her twin sister, Gia, live in Manhattan and are models for a huge agency. They're always traveling, going out, and enjoying their lives to the fullest, which is the complete opposite of me, and I find myself envious of them a lot.

"Yeah, we're in the city for the next few weeks. Of course we can go out tonight. Why? What happened? You sound desperate."

"I am. I'm getting married and I want to blow off some steam before…" I pause and take a breath. "Just…before whatever happens, happens."

"What the hell did you just say? I could've sworn you just said you're getting married, but that's absurd since I know you've never dated anyone in your life."

"Okay, when you say it out loud like that, I sound pathetic. But it's true. Katarina didn't have to marry Santino, but I do."

"Why the hell do you have to?" she asks angrily.

"He said he wants me. I don't know. Some deal needs to go through and I'm a part of that deal."

"Mia, are you messing with me right now?"

"No," I sigh, pacing my room. "I wish I was."

"Okay, just get over here and we'll talk. I'll fill Gia in."

"Thanks, Aria."

Hanging up, I pack a small overnight bag, and as I'm leaving, I pass my mom in the living room. She raises her eyebrows at my bag slung over my shoulder.

"Are you going somewhere?" she asks.

"Yeah, I'm spending the night with Aria and Gia. I need a girl's night. I need to talk things through with them."

When I came back from my talk with Leo and my brothers a few days ago, I vented to my mom straight away. I thought she'd be as angry and upset as I was, but she just sat there and let me talk before she spoke, telling me it was my duty to help the family and that we all have our role we need to step into when necessary.

To say I was angrier with her than my brothers is an

understatement. She made it sound like it was no big deal that I was giving up my choice in who I married for the sake of a business deal. Like my life doesn't matter. My brothers and Leo were at least regretful in some capacity.

"There's nothing to talk through, Mia," she tells me, looking at me like she already knows what I have in mind for tonight. "You've already gone off the deep end and dyed your beautiful hair, ruining it in some fruitless rebellion. Don't do anything else that will alter your appearance and don't do anything that will reflect badly on you or the family tonight."

I ball my hands into fists at my sides to refrain from lashing out. "I already know your thoughts on everything, mother," I grind out. "I need to talk with people who realize how insane this is, though. You can understand that, can't you?"

I ignore her dig at my new hair, because frankly, I fucking love it. After spending a pitying two days in bed feeling sorry for myself, I went to the salon yesterday and spent hours in the chair being transformed from my natural light brown hair to a honey gold light blonde by way of about a thousand highlights. My head was a heavy mass of foils that I was starting to regret until I saw the end results. My mom can say it was an act of rebellion, because it was, but she can't tell me I ruined my hair. It looks amazing.

"Just be careful," she says instead of answering my question. "You don't want to do anything you'll regret or will compromise this family's future."

I roll my eyes. "I'm leaving now. I'll be back some time

tomorrow. Maybe." I shrug. "I may stay two nights with them."

"You'll be home by tomorrow night," she tells me sternly. "You meet Santino the following day and you'll need your rest to look presentable and be on time for him."

I gnash my teeth together to keep my mouth shut and to keep from saying something I can't take back. I've never talked back to my mom. I've never been rude or disrespectful to her. Especially after my dad was killed.

"Sure," I say through a tight throat, and walk right out the door.

I live with my mom in the building my family owns in Manhattan, but Aria and Gia live ten blocks away in a gorgeous apartment that their agency puts them up in as a part of their contract.

Gia opens the door and her jaw drops. "You look fucking amazing, Mia!" she exclaims, touching my hair. Aria comes running over and her eyes widen when she sees me.

"Holy shit, you're a hot blonde, Mia! I love it!"

My first smile in days lifts my lips. "Thanks."

"But you need to tell us everything," Gia demands. "Right now." She drags me to the couch and I drop my bag and flop down, my legs giving way under the weight I feel on my shoulders.

"There's not much to tell." I shrug. "I met with Leo, Nico, and Vinny the other day, and they told me I needed to marry Santino in order for a deal to go through. Santino said he wanted *me* specifically after seeing me at Leo's wedding. He wants me so that Leo won't screw him over in whatever deal they have going. I don't even know what the deal is for. Of course, I'm not privy to that information, but I can be handed over to a stranger that I'm sure expects me to share his bed and be a good little wife to him all because he saw me across the room and wanted me."

I can't keep the seething animosity from my voice, and Jesus, saying it all out loud and seeing their shocked faces has me feeling even more like a piece of cattle to be used as currency.

"I'm so sorry, Mia," Aria finally says after a long pause.

"What the actual fuck?" Gia asks. "I honestly have no idea what to even say right now because my mind is reeling, but I don't think there is anything I can say to make it okay or make you feel better. So, we're taking you out tonight. We're going to go crazy tonight and get you drunk to forget all of this."

"What about your shadows?" Aria and Gia don't go anywhere without their bodyguards. It was the only way their brother, Saverio, agreed to let them sign with the agency and move out on their own when they were eighteen.

Gia shrugs. "I'll make sure they don't say anything to Leo. And even if they do, who cares?"

"You deserve a night of uninhibited fun," Aria adds.

"And maybe there will be a hot guy I can dance with and have pressed against me before I'm in a loveless marriage with a man I refuse to let touch me."

"Have you met him yet?"

"No."

"Maybe he's hot?" Gia offers hopefully. "Did you ask Kat?"

"No, of course I didn't ask her, and it wouldn't matter. But if he is, wouldn't he have found a woman for himself by now?"

She lifts one shoulder. "True. Which means you need a hot man to show you a good time tonight to carry you into your marriage." The evil glint in her eyes has me smiling. "Maybe even do a little more than just have him grind all up on you on the dance floor."

"I've never agreed with you more."

"I'll try not to take that as an insult since I think I have great ideas all the time."

Laughing, I nervously twist my fingers together. I don't want to tell them what I have in mind for tonight. The biggest rebellion I've done in my life up until now was sneak out of my family's apartment and go one floor down to Aria and Gia's when we were in high school. I was mad at brothers for not letting me go on a date with the guy I had the biggest crush on. They told me no, and then scared him so badly, he texted me saying he couldn't talk to me anymore and to not try to change his mind.

I was so mad, sad, and disappointed, but then Aria told me that I don't want a guy who's easily scared off by my brothers anyway. That if they are, then it just goes to show they're weak and not worthy of my time. She told me the right guy will have no problem standing in front of my family and claiming me as his.

I took her words as the true wisdom they are, and have always had them in the back of my mind since. I didn't think the first man to stand before my brothers and tell them he wants me would be one I don't even know.

Tonight, I want to do something for myself. I refuse to have the choice taken from me as to who I give myself to, and who I give any of my firsts to.

I'm painfully a virgin in every way, and I'll bet everything I have that Santino expects to get a nice little virgin as a wife that he'll be able to easily manipulate and keep locked away to have whenever he wants. Or maybe he'll use me as a trophy to keep quiet at his side and parade around like a prize he's won. Either way, I already know he probably thinks I'm going to go along with anything he says for the sake of my family and his stupid deal with Leo.

Well, he's going to be in for a big surprise, because I refuse to give him all my firsts.

CHAPTER 4
Mia

"I'm in love with this dress, Aria," I gush, turning in the mirror so I can see the sequins catch the light. She pulled out a few dresses for me that she thought would look best on me, and I was drawn to this one immediately. It's a long sleeve dress covered in magenta pink sequins, with a feather trim around my wrists and along the bottom hem that hits me just a few inches below my butt. It reminds me of a Barbie dress and I'm completely obsessed.

"Your legs look fabulous," Aria praises, and I have to agree. Especially with the heels I have on that are making my calves look lean and my legs all that much longer.

"And your boobs." Gia whistles, making me laugh. "Damn, girl."

I blow them a kiss. "Thank you. That's the reaction I was hoping for."

I grab the little feathered clutch that matches the dress and we head out. Aria and Gia's regular bodyguards are waiting for us down in the lobby of their building, and they look at each other for a split second before their eyes are back on us. I know exactly what they're thinking from that look – *oh shit, this is going to be a long night.*

"Hi, Jonny." I smile up at him, admiring his green eyes, the sharp edges of his jawline, and his oddly pouty lips that would look feminine on anyone but him. My smile widens when my eyes meet the pair of chocolate brown ones beside him. "Sammy."

"Hi, Miss Mia," Sammy greets, a shy smile spreading across his handsome face. I always found him adorably good-looking, while Jonny was more of a chiseled handsome.

"Now, boys," I start, my eyes darting between them, "tonight is a big night for me. I'm trying to have fun and I don't want you to inhibit that. Got it? No scaring off guys who approach us, and you won't be telling my brothers anything you see. Are we clear?"

"Miss Mia, we cannot promise you that. It's our job to watch out for you. And it's our job to report what we see if warranted."

"Exactly. If warranted. And you're only obligated to do so with Aria and Gia, not me."

"Not true," Jonny says gruffly. "When you're with them, you're under our protection, and we watch over you as we do them."

Sighing, I roll my eyes and look at Aria and Gia. "Should we go?"

"Yes," Gia says excitedly, clapping her hands together, and I don't miss the tick in Jonny's jaw or the narrowing of his eyes when she does. "We're going to Elemental, boys." Gia winks at Jonny and pats his bicep as she walks past him and out the door.

The warmth of the day is gone and has been replaced by the cool night air that lets me know fall is almost fully here. Despite it being October, the days here in the city are still plagued by the warm sun, but the nights are cool, which gives me a taste of my favorite season to come. Winter.

We bypass the line for the club that's already extending down the block, and Aria and Gia walk us right up to the bouncers. They give them a smile, and that's all it takes for them to unhook the velvet rope. "Hello, ladies. Good to have you back. Your usual table is reserved for you."

"Thanks, Carlos. We missed you, too," Gia says flirtatiously, blowing him a kiss as she passes him. Jonny gives Carlos a death glare behind her back and I smile. That man takes his job a little too seriously.

The second I walk through the doors, my smile widens. I've been to a few bars and lounges with my cousins, but never a club like this. The bar takes up the entire length of one wall, with the DJ's booth across the club and the dance floor stretched between it. The other two walls are occupied by U shaped booths and tables with red velvet curtains tied up beside most, with a few of them closed, adding an air of seductive mystery.

On the wood separating each booth are small sconces that have two fake tapered candles with red bulbs that match the dull red bulbs inside the black chandeliers that hang from the ceiling. In between the three massive chandeliers, hangs three large rings over the dance floor that have women spinning and dancing from them like circus performers.

The club is dark and sensual with the black and red color scheme, low lighting, and a dance floor packed with bodies swaying against one another as inhibitions are lowered. It makes me wish I'd taken the opportunity to go out with Gia and Aria more so I could enjoy my freedom while I had the chance.

I feel like I've wasted my life away being someone I thought I needed to be so everyone around me didn't have to worry about me. I sat back and watched my brothers have fun, go out, and do whatever it is they do for the family, all while I was left to take care of our mother who did her best to put on a mask and hide her depression from everyone, except when it was just the two of us.

Shaking away thoughts I don't want to be thinking when tonight is about me and having fun, I pull my shoulders back and glance around as I follow Aria and Gia over to one of the booths marked reserved. Every man and woman's heads turn to look at my cousins as we pass, and I almost feel like a third wheel with them. They're tall, beyond gorgeous, and twins. There's a reason they're such highly paid models and flown all over the world for campaigns and runway shows.

"Well, aren't we special," I say, placing my bag down on the table.

Aria winks. "I made a call after you first called me."

"Do you two get special treatment everywhere you go?"

They look at each other and then both lift their right shoulders in a shrug. "Clubs are always wanting girls from the agency to fill their VIP areas so they look like the hottest club in town."

"And now I get to reap the benefits, too."

"Exactly." She smiles.

Jonny and Sammy remain outside the booth's entrance, melting into the wood with their all-black outfits.

It only takes a minute for a gorgeous girl to come to our table. "Hi, I'm Carrie. I'll be taking care of you tonight. Here's a list of our bottle services for you to look at." She hands Gia the menu, but she doesn't even look at it before ordering.

"We'll have a bottle of Grey Goose with seltzer, cranberry juice, and limes. Thank you so much."

"I'll be right back with that." Carrie flashes us a wide grin and hurries off towards the bar.

"Did you just order us a whole bottle of vodka?" I ask.

"Yeah, that's what you do in places like this. Don't worry about it." She gets a little glint of mischief in her eyes. "Tonight is about you. Go fucking crazy, Mia. Drink until you can't remember why we're here. Drink until you let your guard down and then grab the hottest man in here and dance your ass off. Drink until you black out and need to be carried out of here. For once in your life, you can just let go. Nothing bad will happen. The two oafs will watch over us."

I pull her towards me for a side hug. "I don't want to black out, but thank you for the option."

The waitress comes back with the help of two others. An extra-large bottle of vodka is placed on the table, a bucket of ice, stack of cups, a pitcher of cranberry juice, a few cans of seltzer, and a cup of sliced limes.

"Let me make the first round," Gia offers. I'm not technically of legal drinking age yet, but since we bypassed the line out front without having our IDs checked, I don't think it matters in here. Besides, I'll be twenty-one in just over a month anyhow.

Oh God, will I even be of legal drinking age at my wedding? Because the only way I think I can get through it is with the help of expensive champagne. That thought alone has me grabbing the drink Gia just slid towards me and gulping down half of it in one go.

"Alright," Gia says, laughing, holding her cup in the air. "Cheers to Mia. Her last name may be changing soon, but that doesn't mean she'll ever *not* be one of us."

"And may she find happiness no matter what," Aria adds, and we raise our cups to meet Gia's. "Even if that means needing an extra-large pack of batteries to keep her vibrator at the ready."

My smile is instant. "I could just get a rechargeable one."

"Hear, hear!" Gia shouts, and I finish my cup in another long gulp. "Okay, then," she says on a laugh, her eyes dancing with humor. "I see how it is." She lines up three more cups and pours a shot of vodka in each. She only raises her eyebrows and lifts her cup as a salute before the three of us knock back our shots and then makes me another full mixed drink.

The music is loud and the bass is hitting me deep in my chest. I watch the dance floor while I finish my second drink, seeing everyone swaying and grinding to the beat like the bass is living in their bodies.

I'm not used to drinking. I usually only have a glass of wine with dinner when I feel like it, so the vodka is hitting me pretty quickly and going straight to my head. By the time I finish my third drink and another shot, I'm feeling like my problems aren't weighing me down so heavily.

"Oh, I love this song!" I say enthusiastically when a Latin song comes on. "Let's dance!"

I scoot out of the booth and grab Aria and Gia's hands to bring them out to dance with me. Laughing, I lift my arms and spin around. My hips twist and roll, and it feels so good to have fun without thinking of anyone or anything.

I'm in my own little world, just dancing in a sea of people, and while Aria and Gia have men come up to them and ask to dance, they always decline. That is, until two guys who are beyond gorgeous ask them, and they grab their hands and wrap them around their waists. Hell, I wouldn't be able to resist them either.

Smiling, I continue dancing in my own bubble until a hand

slides against my hip and I turn to see a really good-looking guy smiling down at me.

"Dance with me, gorgeous."

I smile and he takes my hand, spinning me around before settling me against him – my back to his front.

I sway to the beat, and his hand settles on my lower stomach with his fingers spread wide. "You're so fucking hot," the stranger says in my ear, loud enough for me to hear over the music.

I smile at the crass compliment and place my hand over his. He takes it and spins me around to face him, but before I can press myself against him again, another guy grabs my other hand and pulls me away so I stumble and crash against his hard torso instead.

My eyes are still looking at who I was dancing with, and I'm about to argue with whoever just pulled me away from my chance to get what I wanted tonight, but then I see the man who quite literally stole me away from that chance, and my words get stuck in my throat.

Holy shit.

This man is absolutely stunning.

I don't think I've ever seen a more attractive man in my life.

No, I don't think that. I *know* that.

He has dark hair with a sexy curl that's fallen over his forehead, a sharp jawline that's covered in a day or two worth of stubble that I want to rub my hands and cheek against, and striking eyes that are holding me captive. I can't tell what their exact color are because of the lighting in here, but I have a feeling they're something I've never seen before and will never forget.

He's older than me, maybe even by more than ten years, but he has an air of authority and experience to him that is undeniably sexy and alluring.

He doesn't say a single word to me, just keeps his eyes on me as he takes both of my hands and brings them up around his neck. He slides his own back down my arms and sides, and around to my lower back. If I didn't know with absolute certainty I was wearing a dress, I would think he was touching my bare skin with how much I can feel his touch through the fabric.

His eyes are penetrating, searching, and unrelenting with their intensity.

I have no idea what he's seeing in mine, but I can't look away. He's holding me hostage, making it feel like we're completely alone to where I can't hear or see anyone else.

It's just my pounding heartbeat and him.

I weave my fingers around his neck and see his eyes turn molten when I play with the hair at the nape of his neck.

He presses me flush against him and I can feel every inch of him — solid and secure. A wall of muscle that has my core clenching and my blood buzzing with need.

He guides my hips to start moving to the music again, and I oblige with ease, not even realizing I had been frozen in place, too entranced by him.

When I feel his hard cock against my hip, my eyes widen

and my cheeks flame with heat. I don't think he can see my innocent reaction with the red tinged lighting in here, and when I shift against him so I can feel more, his eyes grow darker and his hands burn me through my dress.

I scratch my nails against the back of his neck, causing his jaw to flex and his pulse to pound even harder against my wrist that's resting against his neck. It gives me the urge to find out every single thing I can do to drive this intense, too-good-looking-for-this-world man, to the edge before he gives me exactly what I set out in search of tonight. Because if there's any man in this club that I'd want to give some, if not all, of my firsts to so my future husband doesn't get them, then it's this man.

Licking my bottom lip, I rake my nails down the sides of his neck and grab his shoulders. His eyes dart away from mine to follow my tongue's movements as I wet my bottom lip, and his hands slide a few inches lower so that the tips of his fingers are pressing into the top of my ass cheeks.

My lips part as a small moan escapes, feeling so much of him while not enough at the same time. The sound gets lost in the air between us, but his eyes snap back to mine and hold a newfound gleam like he really did hear me.

Every ounce of him screams 'experienced' and that he knows exactly how to touch and please a woman. And so help me God, I want to be at the receiving end of all of that knowledge. So damn badly.

The songs bleed together and I have no idea how long I've been dancing with my sexy stranger, but with each song that passes, my legs grower weaker and weaker under his gaze until I'm unsure if I can trust myself to walk away from him on my own. Not that I even want to. I know he knows exactly what he's doing to me too, because his grip on me tightens as he starts to lead me off the dance floor, and doesn't stop until my back hits a wall where the lighting doesn't reach his face anymore. He's even more of a mystery to me now.

He dips his head, his lips hovering just above mine.

I need him to close the distance.

I need to know how it feels to be kissed so thoroughly, I lose my breath. I just know that's how he kisses, too. He doesn't seem like a man who does anything half-way.

Sliding his hands down to cup my ass, he squeezes my sequin covered flesh, and I don't even try to hold back the moan that escapes me.

His chest rumbles against mine in response, and then his lips are at my ear. "You can feel how much I want you," he rasps, the roughness to his voice making my pulse quicken further. "And if I were to slide my hand up under this sexy dress, how wet would I find you?" I suck in a ragged breath and bite my bottom lip, his warm breath and dirty words making me even wetter. "Answer me," he demands, his impatience making my smile.

My lips brush his ear as I tell him, "Very."

He groans against my neck, the vibrations traveling through me and settling in my core as he plants a kiss against my heated flesh that sends goosebumps flaring across my skin.

Feeling bold and in a trance of lust, I suggest, "Why don't

you feel for yourself?"

I know we're hidden in the shadows, but that doesn't mean no one can see us or isn't watching us right now. I couldn't care less at the moment, though. I just need him to touch me. I need him to relieve the ache pulsing deep inside of me that began the moment he put his hands on me.

His hot tongue slides up the column of my neck and I tilt my head to give him more access. He rewards me with another kiss below my ear before saying in a rough voice that's fraught with strained restraint, "You do realize you can't offer me what I want the most on a silver platter and not expect me to take it, right?"

"Please," I beg shamelessly. "Take it. Take me. I need you to touch me."

"Fuck," he growls, sinking his teeth into the spot he just planted his kiss, making my stomach quiver and my core clench with the desperate need for his touch.

He keeps one hand firmly on my ass while the other slides over my hip and down my thigh, stroking my bare skin before finally sliding it across the front and up my inner thigh. He leaves a trail of fire in his wake, and I'm practically vibrating with anticipation.

He inches higher and higher, until he's teasing the crease at the apex of my thigh with his fingers, sliding them back and forth along the edge of my lace panties that are hardly a barrier between him and where I want him most. I inhale a sharp breath at how close he is, then choke out a frustrated grunt when he doesn't go any further.

His dark chuckle in response to my disappointment has me digging my nails into the back of his neck.

"So eager," he muses, his lips right at my ear again. "I can feel how hot your pussy is without even touching it. So needy."

I nod my head, my voice eluding me with his brazen words. He cups my lace-covered center, pressing the heel of his hand against my throbbing clit.

I gasp, then moan.

I don't know what's happening to me.

I don't know how a stranger I know nothing about can evoke such a visceral and potent awakening of my body.

"So fucking hot," he growls. "Your panties are fucking soaked. *For me*," he emphasizes on a growl.

"Yes," I sigh, but I know the word gets lost in the music.

He runs his finger up and down the seam of my pussy through the lace, and my head rolls against the wall as I grow wetter and crazier by the second.

I don't feel like myself, and I love that. I don't want to be the good Mia I've been my entire life who keeps the peace. I don't want to keep the peace. Tonight, I want to be a little wild and a lot free.

Once I'm married to that jackass who thinks he can have me simply because he wants me, I won't have the chance to be free.

With thoughts of my upcoming nuptials on my mind, I stiffen at the thought of him touching me. Or, *trying* to touch me, since he probably thinks it's an expectation in the deal. Fat fucking chance. That means this is my one chance to take away something that won't ever be his.

"What happened?" my stranger asks, pulling back to look into my eyes again – searching and probing for the truth.

"Nothing," I say too quickly.

His finger stroking me pauses. "Something just crossed your beautiful mind that made you tense up. Do you want me to stop?"

"No!" I say fiercely, and his lips tilt up in a sly grin. "I mean, it's just…"

"Tell me what's wrong so I can make you feel good." His words are smooth as honey and cover me like a warm blanket, melting me into the wall.

He wants to make me feel good.

Every man in my life right now is doing nothing but bringing me stress and misery, and all this gorgeous stranger wants to do is make me feel good.

"Can you keep a secret?" I ask him, wanting to lay my burdens on someone else for the moment. I'll take them back and carry them with me again afterwards, but for a short time, I want someone else to hold them. Maybe if I tell this gorgeous stranger the truth, he'll think of me from time to time after tonight.

The hand that was gripping my ass loosens and he rubs circles around my bare upper thigh. "I can," he assures me.

"I'm being forced to marry someone I've never met," I begin, and he tilts his head just the slightest, his eyes probing mine even more intensely than before. "But do you want to know an even bigger secret?" I continue, rubbing my own circles on his neck ever so lightly.

My stranger nods once, his eyes gleaming with the collection of secrets he's coaxing from me.

"I have a very overprotective family. Which means I'm going into a marriage I don't want, with a man I don't know, as a 20-year-old who's never been properly kissed or touched in any way, and I don't want him to be the first one."

I don't want him to touch me at all, but I still want to be able to tell him he's not getting the perfect, untouched angel he thought he was getting by marrying me.

"He doesn't get that privilege," I continue. "He doesn't deserve that privilege for demanding me in the first place."

My stranger's lips tilt up in a sneaky grin as he presses a finger against the lace separating him from slipping right inside me. I pinch my eyes closed as desire barrels through me with a renewed ferocity and urgency.

His voice comes out low and smooth when he says, "So, you want to use me as revenge against your husband?"

My eyes widen, surprised that he doesn't sound at all bothered by that. Actually, he sounds intrigued. "He's not my husband yet," I tell him.

"But you want me to touch you," he says, the tongue I want to feel licking every inch of my body wets his bottom lip. "You want me, another stranger to you, to kiss you, touch you, make you come, and ruin you for your soon-to-be husband?"

I arch off the wall, smashing my chest to his. "Yes," I confess, unabashedly laying all my cards on the table for him.

"And just how much do you want me to ruin you for him?

Just how much do you want me to take from you?"

"However much we can get away with right here and now."

His forehead touches mine. "A better man would walk away and tell you no."

"But you're not a better man, are you?" I challenge, already knowing the answer because his fingers haven't stopped stroking me. "You want to ruin me, don't you?"

His jaw ticks and he leans in so close, I can feel the air swirling between our lips when he says, "No, I'm not a better man. And yes, I'm going to ruin you, baby." I melt a little more at the way he says *baby*. "I'm going to make you come so fucking hard, you'll spend every night in bed with your husband wishing it were my fingers inside you and not your own or the vibrator you'll use when he leaves for work. I'm going to make you forget your name."

A strangled moan catches in my throat, and my sexy stranger plasters me against the wall.

"I'll gladly ruin you, *farfalla*," he growls, crushing his lips to mine in a kiss that touches every square inch of my body and permeates into my soul.

I'm fucked.

I've been kissed before, albeit sweetly and hurriedly in a dark corner of my high school during homecoming, and I felt the butterflies of finally feeling wanted. But then he came to school on Monday with a black eye and wouldn't look at me. I didn't bother asking him why, and I never brought it up to my brothers. I already knew it was them and I refused to bother starting a fight. It would've been a waste of my breath. At that point, I was already so used to them keeping boys away from me.

But this kiss…

This kiss is more than butterflies taking flight in my stomach because I'm being kissed by the boy every girl in school wanted. This kiss is a damn fireworks show, setting every nerve ending and cell in my body on fire as I'm drawn closer and closer to exploding.

His fingers that have been stroking me push my panties to the side, and the second he touches me with nothing between us, I moan shamelessly into his mouth.

"So fucking wet. So fucking hot. I knew it." Growling, he kisses me harder and deeper. The fact that I might not know what I'm doing flies out of my head because my sexy stranger is in charge of this kiss. I take his lead and shut my brain off.

I'm lost as his tongue strokes mine at the same time one of his thick fingers slips inside me. My inner muscles squeeze him. My God, it feels good. So good. I've never had anything other than my own fingers touch me, and I never imagined it would feel like this.

"Fuck," he grunts, tearing his lips from mine to drag his mouth across my jaw to my ear. "You're fucking perfect. So hot. So wet. So tight. So made for me."

I don't have any words in response. My brain is mush and no longer in communication with my mouth or body. I'm at the mercy of his hands. And mouth. And tongue.

His thumb rubs my clit and my knees buckle. Luckily, he's

right there to hold me up with the press of his hips so I don't collapse to the floor in a puddle. His dick is thick, long, and hard, and feeling it against my stomach, I wish I could fully experience it for myself.

"I'm going to fuck you with my fingers," he tells me, his voice calm, yet strained. "If I could get away with fucking you against this wall with my cock buried so deep in your virgin pussy that you'd feel the aftermath of me being in you for days to come, then I would."

I whimper, and my core floods with a new wave of need as my pussy clenches around his finger.

"More," I demand, and he chuckles against my ear.

He adds a second finger and I grip his biceps. The hard muscles beneath his black dress shirt are making me wish even more that I could see him better. I want to see all of him.

"I'm the first one to feel your tight virgin pussy squeeze like this. You're squeezing me like your goal is to break my fingers, baby. Like you want them buried deep inside you and you want to keep them there."

He pumps his fingers, working some kind of magic on me that has me trembling and lost in a daze where it feels like the room is spinning as the bass of the music pounds to the rapid heartbeat thumping in my chest.

I squeak out a moan and bite my lip.

"That's it, baby. You're stretching to fit my fingers. Imagine how good it would feel to have my cock stretching you." He licks my bottom lip and bites down on it. "Imagine how good it would feel to have me moving inside you. With you. Claiming you. Ruining you." He bites down on my lip again and I moan, his mouth right there to capture it for himself. "And I would, you know."

"What?" I ask frantically, feeling completely out of my mind.

"Ruin you." He presses down on my clit with his thumb and curls his fingers inside me. Without warning, I explode like a thousand little fireworks are going off all throughout my body.

I don't know if I'm screaming, choking, drowning, moaning, dying, levitating, or what. All I know is that I've never felt anything like what I am right now, and I'm pissed it's going to be a one-time occurrence.

"Fuck," my stranger chokes out, but I barely hear him past the roaring of my blood in my ears.

I blink up at him, and when my vision clears, all I see are his dark eyes already on mine.

"You're so fucking beautiful when you come." He brushes his lips against mine with a gentle kiss that sends a shiver down my spine, and my inner muscles clench around his fingers that are still inside of me. "It was like watching a beautiful little butterfly being set free for the first time."

He rubs his thumb over my sensitive clit one last time before removing his fingers. I whimper against his lips at the loss and feel his own tilt up in a smirk while I come down from my orgasmic high.

Bringing his fingers up between us, I watch as he licks them clean.

"Mmm," he hums. "You're just as sweet as I knew your virgin pussy would be. If I thought I could get away with it, I'd drop to my knees for a full taste, but then your gorgeous face as you come would be seen by anyone who looks over here, and I can't have that." I stare at him, wide-eyed. "Do you think your husband would mind sharing you?" He presses his hips against me in a lazy motion, letting me feel just how much he wants more from me.

"W-what?" I stutter, not expecting him to ask that.

"I want more of you, even if that means I take what's meant for another man. In fact," he says, licking my bottom lip, "it only makes me want you more."

I have no words. I have no response. But my body breaks out in flames of desire again, wanting to feel what he just gave me all over again.

"Yes," I breathe on a sigh, wanting that too.

"You're the most exquisite woman I've ever had the pleasure of touching." He kisses my cheek. "It's too bad this is all I'm going to take from you tonight." Disappointment lances through my chest in a burning strike. I want more. I want to keep feeling this good.

"Oh, one more thing," he says with a wicked grin. Reaching under my dress, his fingers skim over my throbbing core and I bite my lip to keep from moaning at the brief touch on his way to my hip. "These are my prize." He snaps the delicate lace at my left hip, and then my right. "I'll find you again, my little butterfly."

With his parting promise, he takes a step back from me

and brings my ripped panties to his nose before throwing me a wink and a sexy little smirk as he stuffs them into his pocket and walks away.

What just happened?

Did that all just happen?

I didn't even get his name.

I didn't ask a single question before handing myself over to him. I honestly think if he didn't step back just now, I would've let him do whatever he wanted with me. Everyone in the club be damned.

CHAPTER 5
Mia

I haven't stopped thinking about my sexy stranger since the moment he walked away.

When I was able to recover and peel myself off the wall and walk back to the table, I downed a few shots to settle my frayed nerves and waited for Aria and Gia to find their way back to me. They took one look at me and grinned like fools at each other, knowing something happened. Luckily, they waited until we were safely back in their apartment and away from listening bodyguards to grill me about what happened. I gave them a rather PG-13 version because I want to keep it all as a memory that's *just mine*.

I tossed and turned that entire night, then spent all of yesterday doing some retail therapy with the help of Aria and Gia so I could distract myself. I used the credit card Nico gave me years ago without a second thought as to what I bought, figuring I'd earned it for what I'm going to do for the family. What I'm sacrificing. *My fucking future.*

Now, I'm standing in front of the full-body mirror in my walk-in closet, studying my reflection.

Am I trying too hard?

No, I think it's just enough. It's exactly how my future husband will probably expect me to dress and look. Damn it, I wish I could show up in a comfy sweat suit, fuzzy slippers, my hair up in a bun, and no makeup on. But then my brothers would know my game and so would Santino. They'd see it as a childish ploy, and I want to be taken seriously.

I want to broker a deal with Santino and I need him to take me seriously and not see me as a petulant kid who isn't getting her way when I do so. I need to walk in there with confidence and my head held high knowing I hold the power.

He already knows who I am.

He already knows what I look like.

He *requested* me.

Clearly, he's not intimidated by my family, and I hate that that makes my hate for him dim just the slightest knowing he has the confidence to not give a shit what my brothers and cousins might've done to him for being so arrogant.

That puts me at an even greater disadvantage than I already was. I only know his name. I suppose I could've texted

Katarina to ask her if he's attractive or nice or weird, seeing as she was in my position a year ago, but those things don't really matter, do they? None of it will keep my anger at bay when I get him alone today to tell him exactly how I feel about being used as a bargaining chip in a business transaction.

I check my watch and see that I have fifteen minutes until I need to be downstairs. Deciding it looks a little lonely on my wrist, I add a thin gold cuff and two dainty gold chain bracelets, as well as a gold ring on my left middle finger and a stack of thin gold rings with diamonds on my right ring finger. I finish off my jewelry with simple stud diamond earrings in gold settings.

The emerald around my neck glints in the light and I run my finger over it, a small smile pulling at my lips despite everything. My dad gave it to me on the last Christmas before he was killed. He told me he had no idea what to get me, but when he saw this necklace, the green of the emerald reminded him of the time we decided to chop down our own Christmas tree one year. I had gotten so mad because Nico and Vinny wouldn't let me get a turn with the saw. My dad saw me pouting off to the side and made Nico and Vinny let me finish cutting it down even though I struggled by myself with my noodle arms, and then they were mad because I got to do the best part.

My dad was good like that. He never liked seeing me upset and always did what he could to make me smile and happy.

Sighing, I close my eyes and count to five.

My dad isn't here.

Everything that's happened to our family in the past seven years has stemmed from the killing of my dad and uncle by our rival family, the Cicariellos. After that, Leo took over as the head of the family from his father, and my brothers and cousins all stepped up into new roles as well. My uncles decided to step aside and let Leo run the businesses, knowing it was time for the younger generation to take over.

I'm not privy to the ins and outs of everything they do, but I do know that our family is the one every organization wants a piece of and tries to take down. Especially in the last few years.

Closing my eyes, I take a deep breath, and open them again to look at the woman staring back at me.

You can do this.

You're strong.

You will survive this.

He doesn't own you.

You have the power.

I check my watch again and sigh. Six more minutes.

There's a knock at my bedroom door. "Mia, are you almost ready?" my mom asks.

I roll my eyes. I'm the one in this place that has kept track of everything since my dad died, so she should know I'm well aware of what time it is. But of course, I don't dare tell my mom everything I truly wish to.

Grabbing my purse, I open my bedroom door and look my mother in the eye. "I'm ready."

She peruses me from head to toe and back. "Good

choice." She nods, appreciating the relatively modest black dress I chose to wear with sheer pantyhose and black heels. "Although, I think a little color would have been nice."

"I thought black was quite fitting seeing as it's a funeral of sorts I'm walking into, don't you think?"

"Don't be so dramatic, Mia," she says harshly, surprising me. "You're meeting your husband, not burying him."

Regret seeps into me, and I kiss my mom's cheek as I pass her. "Sorry, mom."

"Mmhmm," she hums. "You know, if your father were alive, he'd be proud of you."

I turn around so fast, a wave of dizziness hits me, and I blink rapidly to get myself under control. I'm so sick of being the peacekeeper in this house that I find myself being brutally honest for once. "If dad were here, and I was in this same situation, I wouldn't want him to be proud of me. I'd be mad as hell at him. Don't try and tell me how he'd feel if he were here again. You should concern yourself with what you're going to do when I'm not living here anymore."

"I think I'll survive," she spits back, a fire in her eyes I haven't seen in a long time. She really has no idea how much I've done for her since my dad died. Or, if she does, she doesn't see it as significant enough to make an impact on her life when I'm gone.

I'm once again reminded that I'm simply an afterthought to everyone in my immediate family.

Fine.

Just fine.

Nico can deal with her from now on.

Without saying another word, I walk out of the apartment that's felt like a chain around my ankle for the past few years, keeping me on a short leash. And now, as I rattle the chain, I feel it loosen its grip as the elevator descends and I inch closer to the next chain waiting to tether me in place – Santino Antonucci.

Closing my eyes, I let my mind wander to my sexy stranger, and my body tingles, almost like I can still feel his warm breath against my ear telling me everything he wants to do to me.

His parting words, *I'll find you again, my little butterfly*, ring in my ears as the elevator dings and the doors slide open on the third floor. I know they're all here, waiting for me, but my feet remain planted.

Do you think your husband would mind sharing you?

I'll find you again, my little butterfly.

There will be no sharing and there will be no more seeing.

The doors begin to slide closed again and I open my eyes, staring down the corridor as it disappears. Sighing, I press the button for the doors to open again, and I make my feet move, ignoring the shaking of my legs.

I won't show any fear.

I won't show any nerves.

Only anger. Only contempt.

That's all I have to cling to that feels real right now.

CHAPTER 6
Santino

Sitting in the hot seat in one of the Carfano conference rooms once again, I wait for Mia to arrive. I've waited for this moment for a long fucking time, and I can't wait to see her face when she sees exactly who she's marrying.

My little butterfly dared to spread her wings the other night, thinking she was rebelling, but she's in for a surprise. She probably even believed dying her hair was going to piss me off, but I already know that no matter what color her wings are, my little butterfly will be mesmerizing.

Mia is mine.

Every part of her.

She can't give away to strangers what belongs to me, and I fully intend to make that clear to her real fucking soon.

Leo, Nico, and Vinny sit at the opposite end of the table, and while I love this little game they think they're playing with me, I have far too much excitement running through my veins to just sit here and wait for my woman.

I assume my little *farfalla* is going to show up exactly when she wants to in order to keep ahold of what little control she feels she still possesses over her life. She shouldn't have to worry about that. I want to set her free. I want her to give herself over to me so I can set her free. She'll have all the control she wants then.

Pushing back from the table, I stand, and the three pairs of eyes follow my movements as I walk over to the windows and look down at the unsuspecting people of New York going about their business. I've wondered many times throughout my life what it would have been like to be 'normal' and live a 'normal' life. One where the only things I had to concern myself with while growing up were school, friends, girls, and sports.

As the first-born son to Frank Antonucci, and grandson to Giuseppe Antonucci, I had an obligation to my family that my two younger brothers didn't have to worry about until they turned eighteen. I, on the other hand, took on everything my father and grandfather asked of me from the moment I turned fourteen. I did and saw things a young teenager shouldn't see or have to do at that age when other kids were playing football and trying to bang the head cheerleader.

For me, it was more like watching my dad and his men beat the shit out of those who couldn't pay him, and then letting me have a turn with them when they were less likely to fight back so I could learn. I did bang the head cheerleader before I graduated, but my father's idea of becoming a man was having a hooker sent to my room on my fifteenth birthday because as he put it, *it was time I became a man.*

Jesus fucking Christ.

I close my eyes and pinch the bridge of my nose. I don't need to be taking a walk down memory lane right now.

I shove my hands in my pockets to keep the others in the room from seeing them tremble with anger. They'll mistake it for nerves, and I'm anything but nervous right now. Pure adrenaline is coursing through my veins knowing Mia's about to walk through the door any second now. I can feel her presence before I hear the glass door of the conference room open.

My back is still to her as I face the windows, and while no one in the room says anything, Leo clears his throat after a weighted few seconds.

With a smirk at knowing my girl is probably holding her brothers and Leo silent with a withering stare from her gorgeous eyes, I turn around. Her beautiful face goes from angry, to shocked, to passive, trying to hide the turmoil I know is brewing inside her.

Her eyes don't hide anything, though.

In them, I see the fire she gave me the other night when she thought she was doing something to rebel against me, when all along her fate was to always let me have her firsts. I wouldn't let anyone else have them, which is exactly why I followed her to the club when one of the guys I've had watching her since she met with her brothers and Leo last weekend told me where she was. I had a feeling she'd try something between then and this moment, and I was right. I'm just glad I was able to get to her before she gave what I took to some other asshole in there who wouldn't treasure her gift like I do.

Oh, my little *farfalla*, you have no idea who you tried to screw over. But you will.

"Hello, Mia," I greet, and her eyes flutter like delicate wings as she tries to keep her composure. She's good at it, too. I'd assume her brothers and Leo have no idea that right now, she wants to strangle me before she kisses me. Or vice versa. Or just strangle me.

"Mia?" Nico questions, but her and I don't break eye contact. "Mia," he says more forcefully when she still doesn't reply, and her eyes snap to his.

"Yes?"

"You okay?"

"Yes. Fine," she says. "Do you all need to be here?"

The three of them look at each other, but Leo clears his throat first. "Yes. We need to discuss how this is going to go, and then you can talk to Santino alone."

"Fine." She places her purse on the wooden table with more force than necessary and sits down, immediately crossing her legs. The motion hikes the hem of her dress up, and my eyes feast on her long legs before she pulls her chair closer to the table and cuts off my view.

My smirk grows when her eyes narrow after catching my gaze, knowing full-well that I already know how soft her thighs are under those tights.

"Mia, you and Santino will be married in two weeks. I've already hired a planner that will take care of everything," Leo states, and Mia's eyes widen.

"Two weeks?" she asks, her voice going up a few octaves. "Why so fast?"

"Because we need to merge the families as soon as possible."

She scoffs. "Right. You're losing business by the day and apparently"–her eyes cut to me–"I'm what's standing in the way of solving that issue?"

I can't hold back the grin that spreads across my face, and Mia blinks, dazed at the onslaught of my arrogance. "That's correct."

"Don't smile at me like that, you arrogant asshole," she seethes. "I'm doing this for my family, not because I want you in any way, shape, or form." *Oh, really?* "So don't think this is going to be a real marriage. And another thing…" She turns her attention back to Leo. "You never thought to ask me how I want my wedding? You just hired someone to take care of everything?"

"You want to be involved in the planning?" Vinny asks, surprised.

Mia rolls her beautiful burnt honey-colored eyes. "If I'm

being forced to do this, then I'd at least like to make sure it's done in my style and taste."

Leo opens the folder in front of him and pulls out a business card. "Here's her card," he tells her. "You have free rein over everything."

She slides the card into her purse. "You might regret that."

I have no doubt my little butterfly is going to put a small dent in their bank accounts getting whatever the hell she wants for this wedding.

Mia might see this as a fake, arranged marriage, but me? I can't wait to slide my ring on her finger and call her my wife.

"The invites need to go out in a few days, though, so make sure you talk with the planner on those first."

"Mmhmm," she hums, and my dick reacts, thinking about how she hummed and moaned in my ear as I fucked her with my fingers in the club. "I'm guessing you boys don't want me to know the finer points of your deal, so I'll just excuse myself. See you at the wedding," she throws at me nonchalantly, desperately trying to hold onto her composure.

"Wait," I say as she begins to stand. "We have much more to discuss."

"Such as?"

I address Leo, Nico, and Vinny. "I'd like some time alone with Mia to talk. We can discuss the contract afterwards."

"Fine. We'll be in the office next door."

The three of them leave, each placing their hand on Mia's shoulder before walking out the door.

I flash her a triumphant grin. "We're finally alone."

"You're a lying asshole," she says harshly without filter, and I'm loving this fiery side of her. "You obviously knew who I was at the club, and you still…" She pauses. "I told you…" She shakes her head and looks over my shoulder and out the windows before meeting my gaze again. "You're not going to touch me again. This isn't going to be a real marriage, no matter what you think. You want me as a pawn or prize in whatever game you're playing, and while you'll get me, it'll strictly be on paper only. I don't want my family to go down because I couldn't do this for them, but *I will* find a way out of the marriage at the earliest possible moment."

"I had you begging me for more. I had you begging me to touch you and to take something you didn't want your soon-to-be husband to have. You came all over my hand, wanting my cock to fill you next, and you're telling me you don't want me to touch you again?"

"Yes," she says, but the breathless note of that single word betrays her and what I know she really wants.

"Could've fooled me, *farfalla*."

"Don't call me that."

"You don't like that? Hmm." I rub my jaw. "How about we make a little deal?"

"What kind of deal?"

"I won't touch you." I smirk at her mixed reaction of relief and disappointment. "Not until you beg me to. Then we'll see how real our marriage is." I wink, and her face flushes a beautiful red that I bet would feel warm against my palm if I cupped her cheek right now. Which also has me picturing her ass blooming the same beautiful color after I've spanked her for thinking she could deny what I know she feels for me.

"I'd even bet you're wet for me right now as you remember how it felt to have my hands all over you and in you," I continue. "I know I've been replaying it on a loop since that night, and if it's not your hand, mouth, pussy, or ass taking care of my constant hard-on, then know I'll be jerking off thinking of you and having my cock in all four of those places."

Mia's eyes go from hard and angry, to molten and turned-the-fuck-on.

Fucking gorgeous.

I want to see how they look when I'm buried deep inside her for the first time and she realizes just how much she's been missing out on by denying me. Because I know she'll fight it, which will make her surrender so much sweeter.

Just as quickly as her eyes melted for me, they harden right back up. "I hope you have a good imagination, because that's all you'll be using to get off for as long as we're married."

"I have a great imagination." I nod. "But you'll be begging me to kiss you, touch you, and fuck you within the first week of being my wife. I would say the first day, but I'm not that cocky and you have a stronger will than I first anticipated. I'm not disappointed by that, though. Quite the opposite, if I'm being honest."

Mia scoffs haughtily. "I've gone my entire life without being touched prior to a few days ago. I think I can last a while longer until I divorce you and find a real man to fall in love with and have him touch me as much as he'd like."

"So now I'm not a real man?"

"Not a real man I'll ever consider as a serious husband."

Anger slashes through me, and all teasing is gone when I tell her, "This is a real marriage whether you like it or not, and you will be my wife for however long I say you are. You're not getting out of this and you're not divorcing me unless I say you can."

She raises her eyebrows. "Wow, what a man you are. I can't imagine why you needed a contract to get a woman to marry you."

"I don't need a contract to get a wife, *farfalla*. I needed a contract to get *you* as my wife."

That shuts her up, and her mouth opens and closes twice while she tries to think of another snarky comeback. "You… What?"

Chuckling, I stand and button my suit jacket. Her eyes follow my movements, and when I round the table to leave, I lean down so my lips are at her ear. She stiffens and inhales a sharp breath as she shifts in her seat, confirming what I already knew. "I'll see you at the altar, *farfalla*," I whisper, and she expels her breath in a short puff. "I'll give you the kiss when we're pronounced husband and wife for free. After that, you'll have to beg me for more, and I can't wait for that moment, Mia. I can't fucking wait."

Straightening, I hear her release the rest of the air in her lungs and take another shaky breath in, keeping her eyes straight ahead and not giving me a sassy retort or looking at me again.

Yeah, she'll beg me all right.

I walk out of there smiling like a fucking king and right into the conference room next door, taking a seat in the chair beside Nico rather than across the table and separate from them like I'm being interrogated.

"So, we'll sign the contract the night of the wedding?" I get right down to business.

"Yes." Leo opens the folder in front of him. "I have the agreement drafted here for you to look over."

I take the papers from him and read them over. "It looks like you've got *almost* everything here."

"What else is there?" he asks, his voice calm and level, ever the emotionless Boss.

"You forgot the part where we're partners. I told you I want in on your business, and I want it in writing. The wording in this agreement only states that I give you the trucks you need once you help me get out of my contract with the Gulf Cartel. I'm not handing over any of my trucks if I'm not cut into the business."

Leo stares at me blankly, studying me in a way only a man like him can – cold and calculated, without giving anything away.

"I don't let outsiders in on business."

"We're about to become family, aren't we not?"

"That doesn't mean I trust you."

"After my father, I understand that, but I'm not like him. I want a partnership, Leo. If you trust me enough to ask for my help and marry Mia, then I'd think you can trust me enough to be official business partners."

He stares at me for another long moment. "I suppose. For the explicit part of the business where your trucks will be used, though. You don't get a hand in every aspect of our businesses." I nod my agreement, satisfied with the compromise for now. "But just so you're aware," he says, pausing to lean forward with his palms pressed to the table, "if you do anything to harm Mia, physically or mentally, then I, or either of them"–he wags his finger between the two men flanking him–"will kill you without a second thought and take over every aspect of your family and businesses therein. Including your brothers. Don't think because you're marrying Mia, it means we won't be watching your every move and won't hesitate to take her back along with everything you have. Understand? Or do you need me to spell it out for you in there, too." He jabs his finger towards the papers in front of me.

"I think I'll remember that without seeing it in writing."

"Good. Then I'll have my lawyers amend the contract and have it sent to you to review so it's ready for the wedding."

"Excellent." I clap my hands together with a grin, then hold my right one out to shake on it with the three men.

Nico squeezes mine harder than the others. "Mia will always be a Carfano. She may be taking your last name, but she'll always be a Carfano and carry our protection."

"She'll be protected by me," I inform him, offended that he thinks otherwise. "I won't let anything happen to her."

"You better not."

He lets go of my hand and I stand. "Well, if there's nothing else for today, then I should go. I have a fitting at my tailor for a new tux."

"I gave the wedding planner your information, but here's her card so you can reach out with any questions."

"Thanks." Pocketing the card he hands me, I walk out of there and can't help but look to see if Mia is still sitting in the room next door.

She's going to be a handful, and I can't fucking wait until she's my wife.

It's going to be a long two weeks until I see my lovely, angry bride-to-be again. I'll give her these two weeks to come to terms with it all, but once my ring is on her finger, all bets are off.

CHAPTER 7
Mia
2 weeks later...

I can't believe I'm getting married today.

I'm marrying a man I've spent the past two weeks trying not to think about outside the parameters of hatred and anger.

Of course, I've failed miserably every time my head hit the pillow at night. During the day wasn't much easier, but there's something about the honesty that's found in those moments in the dark when you're trying to shut your brain off and all it does is run through everything you want to forget.

I haven't gotten a full night's sleep in weeks, my mind reeling with 'what ifs' and questions, and wondering how I'm going to survive this marriage.

What if I never went out that night? Would I have a clean hatred for him rather than a mix of hate and desire?

What if Kat and Dante weren't already in love with one another when she was supposed to marry Santino? Does he still want her? Did he ever want her like he's claiming he wants me?

What if I just made a run for it?

What if I refused to marry him at the alter?

What if I marry him and everything he thinks will happen, does?

What if I end up liking being married to him?

Santino knew it was me that night in the club and he still…

I shake my head clear of the memory. No, I can't think about it. Because if I do, then I'm only going to find myself worked up with no outlet.

Fuck him.

I'll bet he thinks he was so clever in tricking me. He played the part of my sexy stranger so perfectly, too.

Arrogant asshole.

From the moment I was able to regain my composure and walk out of that conference room two weeks ago, I've been on the phone with the wedding planner, making sure I get everything I want, sparing no expense. If my family insists we need this arrangement, then I'm going to make sure they get a good dent in their profits from this deal by throwing my dream wedding.

I'd like to think if I was truly in love, I wouldn't care about all the details and I'd just want to be married to the love of my life, like when Kat and Dante got married. Not that a big wedding doesn't mean you're not in love. Hell, Leo and Abri's wedding was in a fucking castle with hundreds of people in attendance.

   But in this fucked-up scenario? I needed to focus on every little detail so I wouldn't have time to think about the man who will be waiting for me at the end of the aisle with that all-knowing smirk.

   Planning the wedding worked to occupy my mind during the day, but at night? Every touch and word that was spoken in a lust-filled haze replayed in my mind, which always led to my hand snaking down my body and into my pajama bottoms to give myself a little relief so I could fall asleep.

   Then last night, Santino sent me a bouquet of white lilies with a handwritten note. I did everything I could to try to have a relaxing night before I got married, but my husband-to-be ruined that the moment I opened the door and saw the massive bouquet in the hands of the delivery man. Then he ruined it even more when I read the note.

   I reach for it on my bedside table and reread it, feelings I don't want to feel rearing their ugly head inside me.

Arranged

Mia, my beautiful bride,

White lilies represent innocence and purity, and while you're no longer explicitly either of those, I'm keeping the purity you handed me so beautifully as the most precious gift I own, and will collect on the rest of your innocence when you're ready and beg me to do so.

That'll be a beautiful day, Mia.

Until then, I'll endure your tongue lashings, knowing that the fire you have burning in you will one day explode all over me. And when that day comes, so will you, *farfalla*. Many, many times.

I hope you've taken these past two weeks to create your dream wedding because it's the only one you're going to get in this life.

Sleep well, my almost wife.

I'll see you tomorrow, waiting for you at the altar.

Your almost husband,
Santino

p.s. – these flowers don't smell nearly as sweet as you taste.

The words swim around in my head until I'm dizzy and surrounded by them.

I close my eyes and take a deep breath in, release it slowly, and then repeat the process until my nerves are settled.

I'm completely disarmed by Santino and I don't know how I'm going to survive this marriage if he evokes this kind of reaction in me simply by reading his words. And God fucking help me for when I'm actually in his presence and he's using that seductive voice of his to tell me all the things he wants to do to me and how I'll be begging him to touch me. I'm going to have to keep my defenses up at all times and make sure I always have something to be angry about, or so help me, I'll be melting at his feet and begging him to touch me before I know it, just like he wants.

Groaning, I throw my arm over my eyes.

In a few short hours, I won't be Mia Carfano anymore. I'll be Mrs. Santino Antonucci, the wife of a mob boss.

I'm even more glad now that we didn't have the traditional ceremony rehearsal and subsequent dinner last night. I didn't see the need for one and told the planner we weren't having one. She was confused, but I couldn't tell her it was because this was an arranged marriage and I had no desire to rehearse walking down the aisle, practice my vows, or sit next to my soon-to-be husband for a whole damn meal without giving in to the urge of stabbing him with a steak knife.

I told her my family and Santino's had to work on an important project to pacify her curiosity, although I'm sure however much Leo is paying her is more than enough to keep her curiosity at bay. I don't doubt she had to sign an NDA when she was hired as well. Lord knows the venue is going to be filled with high-powered men and women from both sides of the law.

The joining of the Carfano and Antonucci families is going to be a public display of unity that sends a message to everyone in our world.

A message of combined forces.

A message I wish I didn't have to be a part of.

I'm being played by both sides in this damn charade and I just want this show to be over with. I've never been the center of attention. I've always blended in to keep the peace, but I know today I'll have all eyes on me, and I'm going to need to dig deep to play my part of blushing bride. All smiles and looks of love on the outside while I'm feeling anything but on the inside.

I have the urge to run, but then I'll have let everyone in my family down, which is something I can't bear. Even more so than marrying a conniving, lying man who only wants me because he likes the way I look.

"Knock, knock!" I hear Aria say at the door. I stayed the night in a suite in the boutique hotel near the venue so I could have some alone time and a place for all the girls to come to this morning to get ready that wasn't in the presence of my mother. I'm not exactly talking to her at the moment.

As soon as I open the door, my cousins – Aria, Gia, Katarina, and Elena – and the significant others of my brothers and cousins come swooshing inside in a rush. Minus Tessa, who is Alec's wife, because she just had a baby and will join us in a little while after she gets her little one up and ready.

Abrianna is Leo's wife, Angela is Luca's fiancé, Lexi is Vinny's fiancé, and Cassie is Nico's girlfriend. Each is beautiful and amazing, and I can see the love they have with their man every time we're all together. They all got to choose their love. I want that chance. I've dreamed of that chance since I was a little girl, yet here I am on my wedding day, standing in a room full of women in love, married or on their way to being married, and I can't seem to get a full breath into my lungs because I don't have a choice and may never get one.

Lightheaded, I grab the handle on the door and flit my eyes between all the women. "I can't…" I suck in a breath. "I can't…"

"Shit," Abri says, rushing forward. "Get her to the couch," she urges.

"I'll get her a glass of water," I hear someone say, while a hand rubs circles on my back.

"Focus on your breathing," Angela says slowly in a calm and soothing voice. "In and out. Feel the air around you and let it fill your lungs, expanding them. In and out."

I look at one of the lilies in my bouquet on the table and focus on the delicate petals. Beautiful. Soft.

I stare at it as I focus on my breathing, and after a while, the short breaths plaguing me start to draw out longer and longer.

"That's it," she says. "Good job, Mia. Just breathe."

I blink out of my daze and look around at all the worried

gazes. "I'm okay," I assure them. "Just having a minor freak out. As to be expected, right?"

"Of course it is!" Gia says, throwing her hands up. "You don't want to marry this jerk, so of course you're going to have a panic attack on your wedding day."

"Gia," Abri admonishes. "That's not helpful."

She rolls her eyes. "Well, it had to be said."

"No, it didn't. We agreed we were going to focus on Mia and making her feel beautiful and special today, and that's all."

"Right." Gia nods. "But Mia also appreciates honesty."

"I do," I whisper. "But I'd like to pretend to be happy."

My backbone is returning by the second, and I feel my defiance and resolve harden into a shell around me to protect me from the stupidly sexy Santino and his belief that he has the power to turn me into a puddle of emotions and hormones that can't control herself. I never told anyone, not even Aria or Gia, that Santino was the one in the club that night.

"I'm going to make Santino regret he chose me," I tell them. "I'm going to taunt and tease him and then never give him what he thinks he's going to get from me. The bastard."

"That's the spirit!" Cassie shouts, clapping her hands. "Make him suffer for a while. Or forever. Your choice."

"You may grow to like him," Katarina offers. "I thought I'd hate him, and I did at first, but that was because I wanted Dante, not Santino. Then Santino surprised me and helped me when I needed someone. He's not a bad guy. And you have to admit, he's objectively handsome."

"Yes, he is. But being handsome doesn't mean he gets a

free pass on forcing my hand in marriage."

"Of course not," Katarina agrees.

"But being attracted to him can be a good thing," Lexi offers. "Fuck him senseless. And if you do it while angry at him"–she shrugs–"even better. It'll make it that much hotter. I was so pissed at Vinny when we first met, and, well…" She smirks. "It was good when I finally gave in."

"Okay, gross, I don't need to hear about my brother's sex life."

"Right," she says on a small laugh, like she forgot I was his sister.

"None of us can know what it's like to be in your shoes right now," Cassie says. "But we're all women, and we all have needs. None of us would, or will, judge you for any choices you make in your marriage. That covers *everything*, okay?"

I hold her gaze and see she's completely sincere in her words, and I appreciate them more than she can know.

My nod comes slow, but her smile is instant when I do, and she radiates this all-consuming, all-knowing, older sister vibe that warms my heart.

"Now, let's get you looking so irresistible, Santino won't know what hit him." She winks. "He'll fall to his knees, thanking the big man upstairs that you're his wife."

I can't help the giggle that bubbles out of me. Santino on his knees for me? Yeah, I'd love to see that. Especially when he thinks it's going to be me who'll be on my knees, begging him for his cock like it's made of gold and he's God's gift to women.

Nope.

Not happening.

I think it'll be him on his knees, begging for another taste of me.

He's the one who demanded I marry him. He's the one who's already touched me and tasted me. He's the one who stole my panties as a prize. And he thinks he has the power to make me weak? He has that backwards.

I'm the one he's weak for, and he's going to realize just how much today.

CHAPTER 8
Santino

"Hey, brother." Emilio slaps my back and grins at me in the mirror. "Nervous?"

"No." I adjust my cufflinks, making sure the Antonucci crest is straight and not upside down. They were a gift from my grandfather when he passed the title of Boss over to me. He told me to always remember why we do what we do and who we do it for. The family. Family always comes first, and every decision I make will be for the Antonucci legacy, not myself.

What he doesn't know, and what no one else in my family knows, is that I made Mia my own personal requirement. I could've brokered a deal with Leo for our trucks that would've been lucrative for my family without involving Mia or marriage, but if I'm allowed one selfish choice in this life I was born into, then I want it to be making Mia Carfano my wife. If she ever came to realize what a weakness she already is for me, then she'd know it'd be me on my knees for her, begging for another taste, and not the other way around.

I pat my chest over the spot where her ripped panties from the club are tucked away in a pocket. Her scent still clings to the fabric and has been keeping me company while away from her.

"If you change your mind, I can always step in and marry her," my other brother, Alberto, offers, stepping up and slapping my shoulder from the other side.

"Not a fucking chance in hell," I all but growl like a caveman.

His knowing grin has me wishing I could knock it off his face, but I don't think Mia wants a groomsman with a busted and bloody lip in our wedding photos.

I don't give a shit, but I want her to have everything she wants today. I've been in contact with the wedding planner, making sure she was giving Mia everything she wanted, including this venue. The Swan Club is on Long Island, and the property has a lake and small waterways with gardens woven all around. The planner told me Mia fell in love with it when she showed her a book of venues, but it's always booked out years in advance.

I, of course, took that as a personal challenge, and with a

single phone call and a wire transfer of an amount the couple that was booked for today couldn't refuse, I got my girl what she wanted. I made sure the planner told Mia that the previous booking simply fell through, though.

I know today is more important than she'll ever know or admit, because she's only getting one wedding in her life, and it's today, to me. The only way she'll get rid of me is if I'm dead and buried, because I sure as fuck am never letting her go willingly once I slip my ring on her finger.

"You actually like her?" Emilio asks. "I thought this was just a business deal?"

"It is." I don't know why, but I don't want my brothers knowing how much I want Mia. I don't want them to see me as anything but their reliable older brother who's always done what's needed for them. They don't know the shit I put up with so they didn't have to, and they never will.

"Could've fooled me with that reaction," he says smugly.

"Besides, why else would she marry your old ass if not because she had to?" Albie asks, the little shit.

I raise my eyebrows. "Old?"

"She's what? 20? She can't even drink yet and you've been able to drink for thirteen years."

"And?"

"And that means you're fourteen years older than her, Santino. I'm only five years older than her, so I should take your place. You wouldn't understand how to treat a pretty little thing like her. You haven't had to win over an innocent woman in a long, long time."

"If either of you offer to marry her instead of me one more time, I'm going to knock you the fuck out."

"Damn, brother, we're just messing with you." Emilio shakes his head and grips my shoulder. "Lighten up."

"He can't," Albie says. "He's about to hand his balls over to a girl who can't even legally drink yet. Which is a shame, since I'm guessing drinking is the only way she's going to get through today."

"Shut the fuck up, please."

"I think you need a drink. Time for a toast." Albie walks over to the wet bar that's in my groom's suite here at The Swan Club, and pours out three glasses of whiskey. "To Santino." He passes Emilio and me our glasses and raises his. "May your marriage turn out to be more than business because you deserve to be happy."

"I second that," Emilio adds, raising his glass.

We're not the sentimental or sappy kind, but I love my brothers and I know they love me, too. I raise my glass and we clink them together.

"Thanks. I appreciate it."

* * * *

Standing at the altar with my brothers beside me, I look out at everyone who's about to witness my nuptials.

My mother is sitting with my grandfather in the front row, and she smiles at me through her usual stoic expression, while my grandfather looks at me with a mix of pride and apprehension. I don't know what he's thinking, but I know he trusts me to make the right choices for our family.

Behind them is a sea of my extended family, and across the aisle are the Carfanos in all their glory, staring me down like I'm the enemy and not the one marrying one of their own.

Weddings are neutral ground in our world, and occasions to be celebrated out of respect. So, sitting in attendance beyond both of our families are men and women from the other two families still in power – Melcciona and Capriglione – and high-ranking members from the New York factions of the Bratva, Triads, Yakuza, and Armenian and Irish mobs.

Sitting amongst them are the corrupt politicians, police chiefs and officers, business owners and CEOs, and even the goddamn mayor of New York City are all here. Security couldn't be tighter if the fucking President of the United States was in attendance.

The second the music changes, I stand up straighter and keep my eyes trained on the French doors that will have my bride emerging from in a few minutes.

From my calls with the wedding planner, I know Mia is only having her cousins as her bridesmaids, and first to walk down the aisle ironically, is Katarina. She's beautiful, but I know I never would have been happy with her. Because even if she wasn't in love with Dante and we did get married to join the families, I still would've seen Mia at our wedding, and with one look at her, I would've known the colossal fuck-up I was making.

Next down the aisle is either Aria or Gia. I can't tell the

twins apart as I've never formally met them or had the opportunity to come to know their differences. The second twin walks down behind her, followed by her last cousin, Elena.

Each one takes their place beside the floral archway that makes up the altar, but I keep my eyes trained on the French doors.

I clasp my hands together in front of me, not knowing what to do with them and needing to hide the fact that I'm unwillingly nervous. I'm nervous she won't walk through those doors or go through with the wedding. I'm nervous she'll look at me with hatred in her eyes and not the white-hot desire she gave me in the club. I'm nervous someone in this fucking crowd will stand up and object when asked just to humiliate me and my family. I'm nervous Mia won't ever forgive me for making her do this.

Fuck, I sound like a pussy.

But no one, not even Mia, is going to stop this wedding from happening. I've never wanted anyone as much as I want her, and she'll come to realize that I'm hers as much as she's mine.

Why is it taking so long for her come out?

Did she run?

Is she freaking out in there?

Fuck, I shouldn't have given her these two weeks by herself. I thought space would help her, but now I'm second guessing that decision.

I'm about to make a move to go and get my bride and

walk her down the aisle myself, but then the doors open, and I'm back to being glued to where I stand.

Holy shit.

Fuck me.

I don't deserve her. Which is exactly why I'm taking her, because I'll never deserve her.

Mia stands frozen in the doorway, with Nico and Vinny on either side of her. She takes a deep breath and her brothers lean in and say something to her, and then they all step forward.

Her head turns in either direction to take in everyone in attendance, and I catch the moment panic sets in, but then her eyes finally find mine, and I will her to keep them on me.

My chest fucking hurts, my heart pounding harder with every step closer she gets.

She's a goddamn angel, covered in pearls.

Our eyes remain locked on the other's, and I will time to speed up so I can finally touch her again, hear her say 'I do', and then kiss her until she can't remember why she was against marrying me. I want to feel her give in to me again, even if it's just a sliver of her defenses coming down. Everyone here will know she's fucking mine.

Mia and her brothers take the final step up to the altar and Nico and Vinny take turns kissing her cheek before Nico places Mia's hand in my waiting one. The second her hand is in mine, I feel a bolt of electricity zap up my arm and go straight to my heart, and by the whisper of a gasp she makes, I know she feels it too.

I told you, farfalla.

I give Nico and Vinny small nods of appreciation, and they give me nothing in return, telling me all I need to know.

I guide Mia to stand in front of me and take her other hand, rubbing my thumbs back and forth over the backs of her hands. Her beautiful burnt honey eyes begin to soften the longer I caress her, and the ache in my chest lessens like she's my balm as much as I'm hers.

I can't see or hear anyone else besides Mia and the officiant as he starts the ceremony.

When it's time for our vows, I regretfully pull one of my hands from hers to get her rings from my pocket. I haven't gotten to give her an engagement ring yet, so I slide her wedding band on first, and then her engagement ring, and I love the little gasp she makes when she sees it.

Fuck, she'll probably make the same sound when I slip the tip of my cock inside her for the first time – surprised by my size and wondering if I'm going to fit.

I bring her hand to my lips and kiss her rings. Her pupils dilate and she bites her plump lower lip, a beautiful pink flushing her cheeks.

I hand her my platinum band and she slides it into place on my finger, the slight tremor in her hands not escaping me as she says her vows. They sound like heaven leaving her lips while mine felt like the greatest honor leaving mine.

Caught up in the moment, she rubs her thumb over the shiny metal that I never want to take off, and this time I can't resist lifting my hand to brush the backs of my knuckles over her soft cheeks to feel her blush.

Mia's eyes fly back up to mine and they're filled with confusion, anger, and something else, but she puts up her defenses before I can get a good read on her. I have another way of finding out how she's feeling, though, because the second the officiant pronounces us man and wife, I barely wait for him to tell me I can now kiss my bride before my lips are on hers.

I kiss Mia with over two weeks' worth of pent-up longing to taste her again. Cupping the side of her neck, I keep her exactly where I want her, and it only takes a moment for her to melt into the kiss.

Fuck, she's the one.

I've never kissed a woman who tastes as good as she does, who makes my body rock-hard in an instant, or has made my heart race like it wants out of my chest and into hers.

I swipe my tongue across the seam of her lips just to tease her and then reluctantly pull away, remembering we have quite a large audience watching me kiss my new bride.

It's the last sweet taste of her I'll get, too, until she asks me for another. But the glazed over look to her eyes and the flush to her cheeks and neck has me believing I won't have to wait too long for that request.

"I missed your taste, Mia," I whisper, and smile when I feel the tremor that runs through her. "And not just your sweet mouth." She inhales a sharp breath and I kiss her cheek.

Pulling back, I smile at our guests as they clap for us, and take Mia's arm to walk us back down the aisle.

Arranged

Bride and groom.
Husband and wife.
Together.
Mine.

CHAPTER 9
Mia

My brain has ceased to work properly.

Apparently, all I need is for Santino to hold my hand, kiss the gorgeous wedding rings he slipped on my finger, brush his fingers over my cheek, and then, oh yeah, kiss me senseless, in order for me to become a puddle of incoherent thoughts.

Alright, so maybe it was the kiss that rendered me brainless and has my legs unstable as I walk back down the aisle. I just made this path a few minutes ago as a single woman, and now I'm doing it on the arm of my husband.

I'm married.

I'm a bride.

I'm a wife.

I'm Mia Antonucci now.

My brain starts to piece itself back together around the end of the aisle, having completely ignored the people clapping for us as we pass them.

They don't know what they're applauding. Or, maybe they do, and that makes this so much worse.

I already am trying to ignore the fact that for a moment as I was walking towards Santino and our eyes were locked, it felt like it wasn't going to be hard to marry him. I was willingly walking towards him rather than thinking of all the ways I can run, ruin him, or kill him in his sleep so I can be done with this farce.

I'm insane.

I'm insane and need a therapist if I thought for even a moment that marrying Santino and getting to kiss him again was a pleasant thought.

Although, there have to be worse things than actually wanting to kiss my husband, right? He could be completely repulsive and make my skin crawl when he touches me rather than flush with heat and leave me with goosebumps.

But desiring Santino's touch isn't a good thing, either.

I don't want to want him.

He saw me and decided I was going to be his whether I agreed or not. He obviously assumed I'd be charmed by an older handsome man with power and a cocky attitude that can only come from an abundance of well-deserved confidence. I never aspired to marry a powerful man, though. My family already has all the power and influence we need, and Santino should know I won't fall on my knees for a taste of something I already possess.

If anything, marrying him is a downgrade.

He tricked me and he played me, and I hate how much I loved everything he did to me in the club. I hate how alive I felt at the thought of fucking over my new husband, and when it turned out Santino was one step ahead of me all along, I've felt nothing short of a fool. But Santino doesn't own me just because we're married now. I'm going to turn the tables on him and make *him* beg for *me*. He's going to be dropping to his knees for a taste of *my* power.

With my new resolve, I look up at my husband, taking in his fine, chiseled features, and think of all the ways I'm going to torture him until he's begging for a taste *of me*.

Starting tonight.

I'll make sure he gets a good eyeful of what I have on under my wedding dress. My dress that I'm so in love with. It has a structured corset bodice and is fitted all the way down to my knees where it flares out just the slightest to allow for the train that flows behind me a few feet. The entire dress is covered in pearls, creating lines, swirls, and patterns throughout that make me feel like I'm wearing both an elegant and a sexy dress.

The dress itself isn't revealing, but the pearls add an indecent sexiness that gives me an unparalleled confidence I haven't felt before. And under all these pearls I'm wearing a sexy white satin and lace lingerie set that was a gift from Aria and Gia this morning. They told me feeling sexy and confident would be my power play move against Santino, and I have to admit, I understand what they meant now.

* * * *

"Ladies and gentlemen, we welcome to the dance floor, the new Mr. and Mrs. Antonucci for their first dance," a member of the band announces, and Santino stands, holding his hand out for me to take.

As he leads me to the center of the dance floor, he says casually so only I can hear, "Do you think our first dance married will go as well as our previous first dance?"

I huff out a short laugh. "No, I don't think it will. Unless you want to put on a show for everyone?"

Santino wraps his arm around me and pulls me close. "No one gets to see you like that but me, *farfalla*."

The song begins and I let Santino take the lead, guiding me around the dance floor, making it seem like I know what I'm doing.

"You can dance," I say, stating the obvious. I'm surprised by how graceful he is. A word I never thought I'd associate with him.

Santino smiles down at me. "I can. I can do a lot of things you don't know about, Mia. But you will."

"I could say the same thing."

"And you should. I intend to learn everything I can about you so that I can make sure you're happy and taken care of in every way."

"I don't need taking care of," I say automatically, even though that sounds like a nice change.

"That doesn't mean I'm not going to," he tells me, and that stupid part of me I need to keep buried flutters with hope that this could be real.

This isn't real.

This is coercion, manipulation, and an exploitation of power.

"It still won't change what we are."

"And what are we?" he asks, spinning me away from him and then pulling me back. I slam against his hard body and he holds me even closer than before, with his arm banded around my back like the bar on a rollercoaster – unyielding and will only release when the ride is over.

"Nothing," I breathe, my lungs collapsing under the pressure building in me.

"If we're nothing, then why did I forget to breathe the second I saw you when those doors opened and you were walking towards me like a damned angel in white? If we're nothing, then why do I know how soft your skin feels and how satisfying it is to see it break out into goosebumps when I touch you? If we're nothing, then why do I know how sweet you taste and how beautiful you look when you come?"

"Santino," I whisper, unable to think straight as my heart is about to beat right out of my chest.

"If we're nothing, then why do you melt for me when I kiss you? Why did my heart suddenly come alive the first time

I saw you? If we're nothing, then why have I carried your panties with me everywhere, every day, just so I could have you close these past two weeks when I knew I couldn't have the real you with me?"

My eyes round in disbelief. "What?"

His smile is small and secretive. "Yes, *farfalla*, I'm a man obsessed. I'm a man who wants you so fucking badly, I've inhaled your scent and beat my cock raw every day. Multiple times a day. I've fantasized about every way I want to have you and how beautiful you'll look under me, on top of me, screaming my name, choking on my cock, and soaking my cock as you squeeze me with your tight pussy."

My core clenches and my steps falter, but Santino's don't. He just tightens his arm around me and keeps us dancing, not missing a beat.

"But I also want inside your brain, Mia. I want to know everything about you and everything you're thinking. I know it'll be beautiful when you finally let me see your eyes in full expression and not guarded."

Staring into his eyes, I'm lost. He's completely serious in everything he's saying, and I'm lost in the depth of his brown eyes, warring with wanting what he's saying and wanting to run out of here. I know my legs won't carry me at the moment though, so I remain in Santino's grasp until the song comes to an end.

He bends me backwards in a flourish of a dip and places a soft kiss to my cheek. "Another freebie," he whispers, pulling me back upright with that sexy little smirk he loves to wear gracing his all too inviting lips. "We're far from nothing, my beautiful wife."

Shit.

I'm in trouble.

* * * *

After dinner, Santino goes off to do his rounds of greetings and bullshitting with people around the room while I take a breath and watch everyone enjoying themselves. I'm glad he didn't try to drag me along, because I don't think I could pretend to be interested in anything they have to say for too long or know how I should act or what to say if they asked me too many questions.

I'm three glasses of champagne deep and staring at my new husband, wishing he wasn't so damn good-looking. Like, really good-looking. As in, I could stare at him for hours and hours and never get tired of the view. Plus, I'm starting to wonder how he would look without that perfectly tailored tuxedo on. I've already felt how solid his body is through his clothes, and I'd bet everything I own he's mouth-wateringly sexy with nothing on.

"If you keep staring at him like that, I'm going to start thinking you like your husband," Aria says, startling me out of my dangerous thoughts of a naked Santino.

I give her a sly, slightly tipsy smile. "We wouldn't want that, would we?"

She laughs and smiles. "No, we most definitely wouldn't."

"But you can't deny he's nice to stare at. Especially when he's not close enough to ruin the view with his arrogant assholeishness that seems to always come out of his mouth." *Except when we were dancing*, I add silently. A mix of sweet and dirty was coming from his mouth then.

"He does fill out that suit pretty well," she admits, and I narrow my eyes at her.

"Don't check out my husband so closely, Aria."

Her eyes widen and she laughs again. "You say he's nice to look at and now you're possessive? You sure you don't like him?"

"I'm sure." I tip my glass back and swallow the rest of the champagne in the flute.

"Are you ready to dance?" she asks.

"I don't feel like celebrating."

"You don't have to be celebrating anything to dance, Mia. I don't want you to waste the night away sitting here. Make some good memories with us."

"Fine," I huff. "But I'll need another glass of champagne."

"Whatever the bride wants, she gets." Aria waves over one of the servers carrying a tray of fresh flutes and plucks off two. "Thank you," she says to him, and then to me, "Now get your ass moving and make everyone see why Santino chose your sexy ass to marry."

"Aria!" I whisper yell.

"What?" She shrugs, then laughs, looking down at her champagne flute. "So, maybe I've had a few vodka sodas before this and my filter is gone. But you can't deny what I'm saying, and if you spend the night sitting alone at your table, then people will notice and they'll assume things. I know you don't want anyone talking about you or today in any way other than how gorgeous you were and how in love you and Santino seemed. Because, honey, that kiss?" She fans herself. "And the way you two were looking at each other during the ceremony? And your first dance? You're either a great actress or–"

"Or what?" I choke out after swallowing a sip of champagne, not wanting her to finish that thought. "Don't even go there. Let's dance."

I practically run to the dance floor to escape further scrutiny and shove my way between Elena, Gia, Cassie, and Lexi, who all cheer when I join them.

"Finally!" Cassie shouts, grabbing my hand. "I was about to drag you out here if you didn't come soon." She lifts my hand and spins me around like a ballerina just as the song the band was playing comes to an end. But as soon as the next one starts, I squeal.

"I love this song!"

Robin S's "Show Me Love" is one of two songs that can get me dancing without fail. The other being Whitney Houston's "I Wanna Dance With Somebody (Who Loves Me)". Both are even better to sing and dance to when you're surrounded by your girls.

This song is quite fitting, too.

But do I really want Santino to show me love? I wanted him to show me *something* these past two weeks, but he left me alone. I fully expected him to show up at my door or…I don't know really, just *something*.

But why?

Why do I even care?

GAHHH! I yell at myself internally.

Fuck it!

Fuck him!

I close my eyes and sing the lyrics with my family like I don't have a care in the world. Because in this moment, I don't.

CHAPTER 10
Santino

"You think you'll be able to work with them?" Emilio asks after we grab drinks at the bar. "Can you trust them to honor their end of the deal?"

"They've never gone back on their word or a contract before. Their reputation is everything to them, so I'm going to trust them. Besides, I have Mia. They won't fuck with me if it means something could happen to her or my ability to provide for her."

"Speaking of Mia…" Emilio lifts his chin over my shoulder and I turn around, my eyes finding my wife immediately.

Jesus fucking Christ.

Her head is thrown back with a huge smile on her face while she spins with her hands in the air. She clutches her chest and sings out the next line of the song – *you've got to show me love.*

Oh, baby, do I want to show you love.

"She's fucking hot, San."

My eyes cut to his. "Shut the fuck up. Don't look at her like that."

He laughs and shakes his head. "Are you going to tell every man in here that too? Because look around, brother. You're not the only one to notice how hot she is and probably wondering where the family has been hiding her."

"I swear to fucking God, E," I grind out, but then look around the room and see all these assholes looking at Mia like he said. The other women she's dancing with are beautiful too, but none of them are as radiant or awe-inspiring as she is.

"Fuck this." I slam my drink down on the bar and weave my way through the tables of guests, all unaware that I'm on the verge of killing any one of them who stares at my wife for longer than they should.

Walking right up to her, I wrap my arm around her middle and pull her against me, her back to my front, and whisper roughly in her ear, "Let's go outside before I kill every man in here for looking at you the way they are."

She turns her head so her lips are just an inch from mine. "How are they looking at me?"

"Like they want to steal you away from me."

"They can look. I doubt you'll let any of them take me

from you."

The possessive growl that rumbles from deep in my chest is primal and almost inhuman. "No one will ever touch you, *farfalla*, let alone take you from me." She blinks slowly, her eyes turning a molten amber for me. I know she likes my possessiveness even when everything she's said to me contradicts that. "Let's go for a walk." She nods her agreement and I place my hand on her lower back, guiding her towards the doors that lead out to the patio and gardens.

The night air is fresh, with a cool breeze that makes the flowers and grasses around us come alive along the pathway. The music from the dining room fades and the soft classical music coming from the hidden garden speakers replaces it.

"It's so beautiful out here," Mia says softly. "It's why I wanted to have the wedding here. I fell in love with it from the pictures the planner showed me when I first met with her. I'm lucky there was a cancellation last minute. Otherwise, there's a very long wait time."

I smile to myself. "Yes, quite lucky. I like this place, too."

She stops walking and looks up at me. "You had something to do with it, didn't you?"

"Yes," I tell her honestly. I could deny it, but I want her to know I'll do anything for her.

Mia tilts her head and studies me, not saying anything for a few seconds. "Thank you."

I smile and she inhales a sharp breath. "You're welcome, my bride."

She turns away and continues to walk along the path, but

I don't miss the small smile she tries to hide.

"I didn't realize you knew anything that was going on with the wedding," Mia says after a minute. "You've been quiet for the past two weeks."

"I told you I would see you at the altar. I wanted you to have the two weeks to plan your dream wedding and knew you might need some space for yourself. But don't for a second think I don't care. About this marriage or about you. If you wanted to talk to me, *farfalla*, all you had to do was call."

"I don't have your phone number," she says, and I smile.

"That's an easy fix, sweetheart." I reach out and brush the backs of my fingers over her cheek. "You would have talked to me if I called? I assumed you'd ignore me, hang up on me, call me an asshole, or try to tell me how you can't wait to divorce me. I didn't want to hear any of that."

"I probably would have done all of those things."

"But you still wanted me to call." She doesn't reply, but I see it in her eyes. She's finally showing me a glimpse of her vulnerability. "I'll make it up to you." I glide my fingers down the column of her slender neck and take her hand in mine as we continue to walk down the path.

She doesn't try to pull her hand out of mine, and after a quiet few minutes, we come around a bend where there's a small dock with a bench that juts out over the lake in the middle of the gardens.

"Want to sit?"

She nods yes, and the breeze blows, bringing with it a coolness from the water, and Mia shivers. I shrug off my tux's jacket and drape it around her shoulders when she sits.

"Oh," she says, surprised. "Thank you."

I squeeze her shoulders and lean in to whisper in her ear from behind, "You're welcome, my bride." Another shiver runs through her, but I know it's not because of the wind this time.

"What deal did you make with my family?" she asks when I take the spot next to her.

"You really want to know?"

"Am I not allowed to know?" she asks, her eyes sharp. "Will that be the kind of relationship we have? One where I'm meant to know nothing, keep my mouth shut, stay in the kitchen, and lay on my back to please you?"

"Mia," I say with warning, "you're neither my personal chef, maid, or whore. Get that shit out of your head right now. And as for the business deal, I simply asked if you'd really like to know. There was no hidden meaning or statement in the question. If you want to know about the deal I made, I'll tell you. I don't want any secrets between us."

"Then I'd like to know."

"Someone is targeting your family. Their trucks, drivers, and shipments have all been under attack for months now, and it's escalated recently to where Leo reached out to me for my help."

"And you'd only provide this help if I married you?"

"Yes."

"Why?"

"Haven't we covered this already?"

"You're telling me there's no other woman you've ever met in your life that you would rather marry than an almost 21-year-old inexperienced girl who's spent most of her teenage years holed up in an apartment with her mother making sure she doesn't dive off the deep end?"

"What?"

"Which part?"

"The part about making sure your mom doesn't dive off the deep end? What did you mean by that?"

"Well, as you know, my father was killed by the Cicariellos seven years ago, and after that, my mom lost who she was. After a while, she was able to fake it enough in front of the rest of the family, but never at home with me. She spent days in bed or on the couch, refusing to go out with friends or family, always giving a plausible excuse. I made sure our home was clean, I cooked every meal, food shopped, ran errands, paid our bills, and sometimes I even had to drag her out of bed to make sure she showered and changed her clothes. I finally got her to go see a therapist a few months ago and she's now on medication, but she still has bad days. It's not like a cure-all. It certainly hasn't changed her negative view of me or gave her the ability to see how much I've done for her."

"You missed out on your teenage years to take care of her. You're an amazing daughter, Mia. Selfless and kind." I can't fault her mother for something she couldn't control, but Jesus, did she not see that her daughter was putting her life on hold to take care of everything and her? Her young daughter who should've been worrying about school and her friends?

Mia doesn't say anything. She keeps her gaze out on the water.

"I'm sorry, Mia."

Her honey eyes find mine again and she gives me a sad smile. "Thank you." She swallows hard. "And I'm sorry about your dad. I don't know why you'd want to tie yourself to my family after what they did."

"My dad did something stupid and paid the price."

Surprise flashes through her eyes. "He's still your dad."

"He knew what would happen by going against Leo and aligning himself with that crazy motherfucker."

"Who?"

"The Alexsanyan family. Albanians. Hovan wanted retaliation for your family killing his brother and all his men."

"They're the ones who shot up Giorgio's."

"Yes." I nod. "Right after my dad and I left the lunch we had for me to meet Katarina for the first time."

"Right," she grumbles, and the slight pout of her lips makes me smile.

"No need to be jealous, my beautiful bride. I didn't feel an ounce for her what I feel for you. That was a deal made between our fathers years prior to bring our families together."

"Kat is beautiful."

"She is," I agree, and Mia's pout grows. "But beauty doesn't equal attraction. And baby…" I take her hand and bring it to my lips, placing gentle kisses across her knuckles. Her breath catches. "We both feel this. Don't deny it. I'm a man who knows what he wants. I'm 34, *farfalla*. I've been with plenty of women and can say with absolute certainty that none of them hold a candle to you."

"I'm not going to beg for you, Santino," she says, lifting her chin defiantly. "I've never begged for anything in my life, and I don't intend on begging a man who's been with plenty of women and can get any woman he wants. In fact, I think it'll be *you* begging *me*, husband."

Fuck. Me.

Her sassy, confident attitude is so fucking hot.

"Is that what you'd prefer?" I ask her, lowering my voice. "If I begged you right now to kiss me? Begged you to take my cock out and lick it from base to tip before sucking me into your hot wet mouth until I come down your throat and coat your insides with me like I'm marking my territory? You want me to beg you to lift your dress up and spread your legs so I can see how wet you are for me, and then beg you for a taste of your sweetness?"

Her throat works around a hard swallow and her lips part as her breathing accelerates.

"Because I can change the rules, *farfalla*. I'll beg you for all of that, but then you'll have to beg for my cock when you realize you need more than my mouth and fingers. You'll feel an ache deep inside you that only my cock can reach when I'm stretching you and filling you as far and as much as you can take." Mia's eyes glaze over. "So, tell me, do you want me to change the rules?"

She nods her head without hesitation and I grin triumphantly.

"Then let me kiss you, Mia. I need to taste your sweet lips again like I need my next breath. I'll go fucking mad if I don't kiss you right now."

Her lips tilt up in a sly little grin like this was her plan all along.

"Please," I add, and her grin widens.

"Well, since you begged so nicely…"

I cup the side of her neck and run my thumb along her jawline, coaxing her to lean into my touch as her eyelids flutter closed. I slowly lean in, touching my forehead to hers and gliding my nose down the bridge of hers, loving the hitch in her breath as I tease her.

I plant soft kisses to each of her cheeks and hover my lips above hers, ever so softly kissing the corners of her mouth.

"I thought you wanted to kiss me?" she asks desperately, and I chuckle.

"I do. Badly. But I thought you might need a warm-up."

"I don't," Mia says urgently, grabbing the back of my neck and pulling me to her lips. She kisses me with as much passion as I feel and I couldn't feel more fucking free or high knowing *she's* kissing *me*.

I let her have control for about five seconds before I take over and take from her everything I begged for.

I sweep my tongue across her lips and she grants me access, meeting my tongue with hers. We both groan on contact and I suck her tongue between my lips, her sweet resounding moan making my dick throb.

I nibble on Mia's bottom lip and then her upper lip,

basking in the moans and sighs leaving her and going straight into my mouth for my hungry consumption. I could live off her pleasure like the fucking fiend for her I am.

She grips my hair and fuses her lips to mine, ensuring I give her exactly what she wants, and *fuck me*, a greedy and eager Mia is definitely going to be my undoing in this life and the next.

But then Mia pulls back, panting. "We should get back." Our ragged breaths fill the air between us before she adds, "Shouldn't we?"

"It's our wedding. We can do whatever we want."

"Then we should get back." I don't miss the tinge of regret in her decision, but I don't want to push her too far, too soon. We have plenty of time. Besides, I plan on begging her for another kiss later when we're finally alone at home. A chance to kiss her *everywhere*.

CHAPTER 11
Mia

I *like my husband.*

The thought hits me like a punch to the stomach, chest, face…everywhere.

Has Santino hypnotized me? Brainwashed me?

I was angry at him not too long ago, yet here I am, holding his hand as we walk back through the magical gardens to our wedding reception after we kissed each other like we were on fire and the other's mouth was the only way to smother the flames. And that was *after* I told him about my mom, which is a topic I've never talked about or told anyone about before.

Am I in an alternate universe?

Too much is swirling inside me and I can't think straight when he's touching me. Hell, his voice and simply being near me is enough to unhinge me.

I try to pull my hand away from his when we reach the patio and I see there are people from the reception outside getting some air, but Santino isn't having it.

"Don't," he scolds, squeezing my hand. He brings our joined hands to his lips and kisses my knuckles gently like he did during the ceremony. "It's okay to show people you like your husband."

"Or pretending to," I counter, to which he growls in response.

"Whatever you have to tell yourself, *farfalla*. But there's no pretending or faking how you react to me. I know, Mia." He leans in and kisses my cheek, and then that spot below my ear that sends a shiver down my spine and has heat pooling in my core. "I know," he repeats.

My brain ceases to work to come up with a good response, so I focus on keeping my breathing even and not stumbling in my heels as we continue to walk across the patio and back inside the venue.

"It's time to cut the cake!" our wedding planner says urgently. "I was worried you two had left early, but was informed you were seen headed out into the gardens. I'm just glad you're back in time."

"I wouldn't want to mess up your schedule, Janine," I say with a sweet smile despite my annoyance. If I wanted to leave my wedding early, then I could damn-well leave my wedding early.

Janine takes a deep breath and pulls her shoulders back. "I'm sorry. I just received a lot of questions about your whereabouts from both of your mothers and then your brothers," she directs at me. "I'll have the band announce the cutting of the cake after their next song." Turning on her heel, she signals the band and then makes her way to the kitchen.

"Where did you two go off to?" Nico asks, walking up to us with his arm slung around Cassie.

"Admiring the gardens," Santino answers cooly.

Nico lifts his glass of whiskey to his lips, but pauses when his eyes spot my hand in Santino's. "That better be all you were admiring."

"Nico," Cassie warns, sliding her hand up his chest. "It's their wedding day. I'm sure Mia just needed some fresh air to relax and clear her head. It's been an overwhelming day with all eyes on her." Cassie throws me a quick wink to show me she's got my back.

"Mia should be used to having everyone's eyes on her wherever she goes with how beautiful she is," Santino says smoothly, his voice soothing all my nerves.

Nico rolls his eyes and Cassie grins from ear-to-ear. "Let's go sit, Nico. They're clearly okay."

I give my brother a small, reassuring smile, and Santino squeezes my hand as they walk away.

"What did he think I was going to do? Steal you away in the middle of our wedding reception, never for you to be seen again? Or steal you away to try to fuck you five seconds after getting my ring on your finger?"

"Probably." I shrug, and Santino laughs, surprising me. I openly gape at his handsome face as it morphed from serious and chiseled to open and boyish.

Damn it, I like both versions of him.

"Let me introduce you to my brothers. But I have to warn you, Alberto offered to marry you instead of me just this morning, so he might say something stupid."

"What? Why?"

"He told me I'm an old man who wouldn't know how to handle your youth and innocence. He thinks I don't have much to offer you."

"Do you agree with him?"

"No," he scoffs. "My brothers don't know me like they think they do."

I have so many questions I want to ask him, but hold them in as he walks us over to his brothers. "Emilio and Alberto, I would like to formally introduce you to my wife, Mia Antonucci."

I can't deny the shot of pleasure that spears me at the sound of my new name when he says it.

"It's a pleasure to meet you," Emilio says, taking my free hand and kissing the back of it.

Santino growls his displeasure, but his brother's touch and kiss doesn't elicit a reaction the way his does. "You as well."

"If our brother gets too boring for you in his advanced age, let me know and I'll take you out for a good time," Alberto says, taking my hand from Emilio and kissing it, too. "And you can call me Albie. All my friends and family do."

I sense Santino tense and know he wants to say something to his brothers, but I squeeze his hand and beat him to it. "That's nice of you to offer, but Santino has already proven to be far from boring. However, I'll let you know if that changes."

Emilio and Albie laugh. "Welcome to the family, Mia," Emilio says with a huge grin.

"Thank you." I smile back, then peer up at Santino who's looking down at me with that stern and chiseled look back on his face. My smile fades and I want to ask him what's wrong, but that's the moment the band announces that it's time to cut the cake, so I don't get the chance.

Standing behind me, Santino covers my hand with his and we cut through the bottom tier of the cake.

"Did you know this part of the ceremony symbolizes our unity and strength coming together and us completing our first task together in our new life?" he whispers in my ear. "And when I feed you this bite," he continues, murmuring so only I can hear him as he breaks off the end of the slice we just cut and holds it up to my lips, "it symbolizes my first act of providing for you. Keeping you full in all ways will be an honor, my wife." He smiles and winks, so I make sure to swirl my tongue around his fingertips to get all the buttercream off, and his smile falters while his eyes heat.

Feeling bold, I lick my lips and throw him a wink before I feed him a piece of cake. He doesn't get the chance to tease me back, though, because I pull my hand away the moment he bites into the cake and suck on my thumb and forefinger to clean them off.

His eyes turn molten. "You like playing with fire, don't you?"

I lift one shoulder in a casual shrug. "I've never been let out to play before, so I don't know."

"Fucking Christ," Santino grumbles, and a giggle bubbles out of me that has his eyes heating further.

The band starts to play another song as the cake is wheeled back into the kitchen to be cut, and Santino takes the opportunity to insist I dance with him.

"I think I need to sit down," I counter. I don't think I can handle having his arms around me again right now. Not after the kiss in the garden.

Today is not going how I thought it would and it's confusing. My hatred for Santino is waning every second longer I'm near him, and I'm afraid for the day when I may not hate him anymore.

CHAPTER 12
Santino

"Time to go, my bride," I tell Mia, and she nods, twisting her cloth napkin in her hands on her lap.

Standing, we make our way around the room, stopping by the table where her brothers and cousins are seated. Mia says her goodbyes to the girls while deliberately avoiding the men.

I love the backbone my girl has. I honestly think I would've hated it if she was too agreeable or eager, or even indifferent, in marrying me. I already proved to her we have the explosive chemistry to be compatible, but I like that I have to earn her heart and her body. And when I do, I'll do everything in my power to keep them safe and keep her trust.

Nico and Vinny stand. "Can we talk to you for a minute, Mia?" Nico asks.

Mia pauses, contemplating if she should. "Fine."

"Alone," he emphasizes, his eyes darting to mine and then back to his sister.

I place my hands in my pockets and watch the three of them walk out of the room for more privacy.

"I'd like a word as well," Leo says to me.

"Alright."

"Let's go outside."

The night air is refreshing and I want whatever this little talk is going to be about to be over quickly so I can get Mia home.

"We signed the contract earlier," Leo says, stating the obvious.

"We did." We signed it before dinner in one of the spare rooms here. I refused to sign before the ceremony.

"I reached out to the Melccionas and we're set to meet with them on Monday."

"Good thing I didn't have a honeymoon planned."

Leo's face turns murderous. "Don't make me wish I killed you and took what I need from your family instead of this deal. I'm entrusting my cousin to you and saw today that I think you genuinely care for her in some capacity, but if you harm one single hair on her head or force her into anything, I will rip up our deal, rip out your throat, cut off your dick, and then burn your body in front of your family so they know what you did."

"Jesus, I was making a joke, Leo. But even if I was taking

Mia on a honeymoon, I would never force her to do anything just because we're married. I'm not a fucking animal. Whatever happens between us from here on out will be because Mia and I want it to."

"Good," he says, his jaw still clenched.

"But don't threaten me or my family like that again. I stood next to my father when you gave the order to kill him and I watched him die. I haven't forgotten what you're capable of, but I'm not my father, just as you're not yours. I respect you, Leo. You've always been a man of your word, and you may not know it yet, but I am too."

"We'll soon find out. Trust is earned with me, and all it takes is one mistake for it to be broken. I don't give second chances."

"Same with me."

"Good to know."

Leo holds his hand out, and as we're shaking hands, Mia bursts out onto the patio, her face a mix of angry and annoyed.

"I'd like to leave now, Santino."

"Of course. Leo, I'll see you Monday."

He nods, but doesn't say anything to Mia, probably already knowing what her brothers said to make her so upset.

I place my hand on her lower back and walk us along the path that circles the venue rather than go back through the reception and room full of people.

"What did they say to you?" I ask, trying to keep my voice calm so I don't give away how much I want to go back in there and throttle her own family for upsetting her on her wedding day of all days.

"Let's just get out of here."

We make it to the front of the venue and Mia stops short. "I didn't," she starts to say, then stops, her wide eyes on the vintage Rolls Royce I rented for us. "Did you?"

"I did. You planned everything, but when I asked Janine about our ride home, she said you hadn't requested anything."

"I didn't realize I needed to. I didn't think of it."

"Well, I did. I thought you might like it."

"I do." She smiles up at me and my fucking heart swells in my chest.

The driver steps out and rounds the car, opening the rear door for us.

"Thank you," Mia politely says to him before she maneuvers into the car. I pick up the train of her dress and lift it in behind her, and the sweet smile she gives me in return has my heart doing that weird stammering it's only done since she's come into my life.

Mia is quiet for the first ten minutes of our drive, her eyes glued out the window. "This isn't the way to the hotel," she finally says.

"No, it's not. We're not going to the hotel."

Her head whips towards me. "Where are we going?"

"Home."

"Home?" She eyes me speculatively. "And where's that?"

"Manhattan. I wanted to start our marriage off where we'll be living, not in a hotel where a lot of our family and other guests are staying."

"You're taking me to your apartment in the city?" Her voice is laced with panic.

"Yes. It's your home now, too."

Mia rolls her lips between her teeth. "I had important belongings in my hotel room."

"I've already got that sorted. Everything is already waiting for you at the apartment."

She goes back to looking out the window and I wish I could read her mind.

"What did your brothers say to upset you?"

She twists her fingers together in her lap and she shakes her head. "They pulled me aside to talk to me about us being…" Pausing, her eyes dart to mine and then back out the window. "Intimate," she finally finishes.

"Excuse me?" I grind out, pissed off. "What the fuck did they say to you exactly?"

"They were reiterating to me that I don't need to do anything I don't want to do and I shouldn't let you touch me. They were speaking to me as if I don't have a mind of my own and am perfectly capable of keeping you in line."

My anger dissipates when I realize what she just said, and smile at her in disbelief. "Excuse me? Keep me in line?"

"Yes," she says smugly. "Don't question my capabilities to do so when I've already gotten *you* to beg *me*. Besides, I'm more than certain you won't force me to do anything because you seem to have a begging kink. You don't want easy."

"No, I don't," I rasp. "And you're right." I lean in, brushing the tip of my finger along her jaw and bottom lip. "I may have a begging kink. I didn't before you, though."

"It's good to know I'm special," she whispers.

"Oh, you're special, *farfalla*. Very special." Mia licks her lips and my eyes follow her tongue, wanting her to lick my lips in the same way. "I can't wait to find out what other undiscovered kinks I have with you."

Her eyes are on mine and her breathing is steady, but I can see her pulse pounding in her neck, and I want to feel it beating against my tongue as I lick up the column of her neck to her sweet spot below her ear that I know drives her crazy. For now, I slide my finger down her throat and over to her jugular. Her pulse picks up speed at my touch and I look at her expectantly.

"I love feeling your heart rate spike when I touch you, *farfalla*. Do you want to feel mine?"

Mia raises her hand slowly and brings it to my neck to mimic mine. Her cool, gentle touch on my heated skin has me clenching my jaw so I don't scare her away by either slamming my mouth against hers or hauling her up onto my lap and burying my face in her neck.

"Do you feel it?" I ask, and she nods. "It's because of you. I told you, you're special."

"I'm sure plenty of women have spiked your pulse, Santino," she whispers.

"Not like this. Never like this." She gives me a soft smile. "Let me kiss you again," I plead. "I want you to feel what happens to my pulse when I do."

"Yes," she sighs, and I don't waste any time.

I cup Mia's neck so I can feel her pulse as I press my lips to hers, loving the jump in her heart rate the moment they do. She presses her fingers into my neck to feel mine in return.

I lick the seam of her lips and she opens for me, her tongue sliding against mine in a sensual kiss that has my cock stiffening in an instant.

She has that effect on me, and I fucking love it.

Our kiss is slow and sensual, and carries too many promises to count.

I pull away before I lose control, resting my forehead against hers. "Do you feel it, Mia?"

She nods, her fingers pressing into my neck. "It matches mine, doesn't it?" she asks, the whisper of her words brushing my lips.

"It does." I kiss the corner of her mouth. "But I think yours is beating a little faster." I kiss the other corner. "Which I like," I admit, placing a barely there kiss to her lips.

I take her hand from my neck and kiss her knuckles before weaving our fingers together and placing our joined hands on my thigh for the rest of the drive back into the city.

CHAPTER 13
Mia

Stay strong, Mia.

Santino needs to stop being sweet. He needs to stop touching me. He needs to just…stop.

He keeps ahold of my hand the rest of the way into the city, and even when we pull up to the curb outside of his apartment building, he gets out while still holding my hand and then helps me out.

"Congratulations, Mr. and Mrs. Antonucci," our driver says, bowing at the waist.

"Thank you." Santino gives me a little smirk, and when we're a few steps away, he says, "I'll never get tired of hearing that."

"I don't think I'll ever get used to hearing it."

He wraps his arm around my waist after we enter the building, plastering himself against my back to whisper seductively in my ear, "I'll say it every chance I get so you get used to it, Mrs. Antonucci." He kisses me in my favorite spot and releases me from his hold.

I dart across the lobby as fast as my heels will carry me and glare at my too-sexy husband when I hear him chuckle behind me.

"You'll never be able to run faster or get far enough away from me, my bride. I'll always catch you. I'll always find you."

"You're starting to sound a little obsessed, my husband."

We step into the elevator and Sabtino crowds me into the corner after pressing in the code for the penthouse floor.

"Starting to? I thought I've made it crystal clear that I'm totally…" He runs a finger up my arm. "Completely…" His finger slides across my clavicle. "Utterly…" His finger swirls around the hollow at the base of my throat. "So far gone obsessed with you."

Santino cups the front of my throat in a possessive embrace. "I made sure you married me, Mia. I made sure you were legally bound to me before another man could even think of asking you out. I already know no other man will see you as I do. Will want you as I do. Will give you the world like I will. Will make you feel as desired as I will. Will worship you like I will. Will make you come harder, longer, or more intensely than I will. Does that sound like I'm *just* starting to be obsessed with you, Mrs. Antonucci?"

I'm dizzy. He's so intense.

"No, it sounds like you're already there."

"I am, *farfalla*." Santino strokes the side of my neck with his thumb.

"Why do you call me that?" I ask softly.

"Because you're beautiful, delicate, and unique. The world is in awe of you whenever you let it see you. You've been hidden away for too long, and it's time for you to fly."

That's the most beautiful thing anyone's ever said to me.

I try to lift up on my toes to kiss him, but his hand around my throat keeps me where I am.

"Do you need something, *farfalla*?"

He won't get any asking or begging from me, so I just shake my head no, which has him smiling like a fool.

Santino leans in closer, bringing his lips to within an inch of mine. "I know exactly what you want, Mia, and this time, and this time only, I won't make you say it."

The elevator dings and the doors slide open, breaking the moment and giving me the much needed excuse to push him away and get some air in my lungs. Air that isn't contaminated by his manly, musky cologne that has me wanting to kiss him senseless, bury my face in his neck, inhale deeply, and then lick him all over.

Jesus.

Shit.

Fuck.

I need out of this elevator.

There's a sign on the wall that says penthouse one is to the right, and two and three are to the left.

"This way," Santino says, nodding to the right as he holds the elevator open with his arm. "My brothers live in the other two on this floor. If you ever need anything and I'm not here, you can always knock on their doors. I'll leave you their phone numbers as well."

"Okay." My mind is reeling with everything that leaving this elevator and entering his home will entail.

Santino unlocks his front door and holds it open for me. "Welcome home, Mrs. Antonucci."

My throat immediately clogs with emotions and I swallow them down. I need to get back in control of this situation.

"Would you like a tour?" he offers.

"Maybe later. I'd like to get out of this dress first."

"If you're sure. It's a beautiful dress and it suits you perfectly."

"Thank you." I turn my head and look at him over my shoulder. "I'll need a little help, though. There are a lot of buttons and I can't reach them."

Santino steps up behind me and runs a finger over the line of pearl buttons that follow my spine. "It'd be my pleasure," he says, his voice dropping to a dangerously deep level with a roughness that scratches an itch deep inside me.

His fingers deftly undo each button, slipping the pearls free from the elastic loops around them. It takes a few minutes for him to make it down to the base of my spine, and when he does, he glides a knuckle down the same path.

Before he can comment on the lingerie he sees I'm wearing, I hold my dress to my chest and look back at him. "I just need a few minutes in the bathroom."

Clearing his throat, Santino nods and points to the hallway off the living room. "The first door on the right."

I bite my lip as I walk away to keep the grin off my face, knowing his eyes are still on me.

I open the door he directed me to, but instead of a bathroom, I find myself walking into what I think is the master bedroom. It's done up in blacks and creams, and I've never seen a more inviting bed with a fluffy comforter that resembles a cloud. The huge curtains are pulled open, giving me a view of the city very similar to my old one, just higher up.

Not wanting to ruin my dress in any way, I shimmy it down my body and step out of it, then drape it over an accent chair beside a small table where a carafe of water and a clean glass sits.

During the reception, going to the bathroom in my dress required the help of two other people, so I only went twice, and now my bladder is screaming at me to relieve it. I keep everything else on, including my heels, and walk across the bedroom to the en suite.

I flip the light switch on and gasp. I don't know what I expected, but a lavish black and white marble bathroom with a massive clawfoot tub that's almost double the size I'm used to, a shower that looks like it could fit eight people, and a double vanity with enough counter space to hold all my products and then some. It's beautiful, and I love the gold accents and fixtures that stand out against all the black and white.

After using the toilet, I stand in front of the mirror and take out the pins holding my hair up. I run my fingers through the curls to break them up and fluff them out a little.

I have to admit, I've never looked or felt sexier than I do right now. I've never had a need for lingerie, so I'm glad Aria and Gia thought to buy me this set so I'll feel sexy and confident rather than a shy virginal bride being married off to an older man to be defiled.

I want Santino to see me like this.

I want him to drop to his knees and beg me to let him have a taste of what no one else has.

I want him to tell me all the dirty things he's going to do to me while he's looking at me with those eyes that hold the depth of space and the heat of the sun.

Stepping out of the bathroom, I find my new husband walking into the bedroom, and he halts, those deep chocolate eyes raking over my body from head to toe and back. Then again slower, drinking in everything I have on.

They start on my pearl encrusted Jimmy Choo heels, then follow up my legs that are covered by thigh-high nude stockings with a white lace trim and held up by a white satin garter belt and straps. He pauses at the juncture of my thighs where my white satin panties sit low on my hips, then moves up to the garter belt around my waist, and keep going up to my strapless longline satin bra with bone ribbing and a lace trim around my ribs and the cups.

Finally, his eyes roam over my chest, neck, and hair before he meets my eyes, and I see that his are filled with raw, hot desire.

I'm emboldened by his reaction to me and the fact that I seem to have rendered him speechless, and decide to ask, "What are you thinking right now?"

"Honestly?" he prefixes, and I nod. "Right now, I'm thinking that I'm the luckiest man on this goddamn planet because you're real. You're really standing in front of me looking like a goddamn Victoria's Secret Angel, and you're *my wife*," he growls. "You're a literal dream come true, Mia."

I walk towards him, swaying my hips with each step. Reaching up, I pull on his bowtie to untie it, and he looks down at me through hooded, lust-filled eyes, and my pussy clenches, wanting him to touch me more than anything right now.

"It's your turn to tell me what you're thinking," he says in his deep, sexy voice.

"Honestly?" I ask, and he nods. "I was thinking how I want you to get on your knees and beg me to let you touch me."

"And then?" he prompts, his voice strained.

"And then you'll beg me to let you undress me."

He swallows hard. "And then?"

"And then you'll beg me to let you kiss me all over."

"All over? Anywhere in particular?"

"Here." I skirt my finger over my breasts. "And here." I slide my finger down my stomach and swirl it over my mound.

Santino shrugs off his tuxedo jacket and tosses it over to

the bed. Without a word, he sinks to his knees before me and looks up at me, his eyes alive and dancing with a sparkle of mischief and determination. He's so tall, that even on his knees, his head is level with my chest.

"Mia, my beautiful bride, I don't deserve you, but I know I can be everything you need. Let me show you. Let me touch you. Let me unwrap you like the precious gift you are. Let me kiss my way around your perfect body, ending at your sweet pussy where I'll kiss you until you're screaming my name and coming all over my face. Please let me. I'm fucking begging you," he pleads. "Will you let me?"

I think I black out for a second, because hearing Santino say all that while looking up at me from his knees has my mind spinning.

I nod my head slowly. "Yes," I whisper, and Santino slides his hands from the backs of my thighs down to my ankles.

"As sexy as you look right now, and as much as I'd love to rip your panties off and have you leave the rest on, I need you naked tonight. I need to see all of you."

Santino lifts my left foot and slips my heel off, and then the right. He slides his hands back up my legs and unclips my garter belt straps from my stockings, then slowly – oh, so slowly – peels them down and off me.

"These legs," he muses, lifting my leg and kissing his way from my ankle to my knee. "I can't wait to have them wrapped around my shoulders while I eat my dessert."

My chest rises and falls with heavy breaths, unable to control my breathing or my reactions to him.

Santino continues to kiss his way up each of my inner thighs, stopping short of where I need him most each time.

My garter belt is held together with hook-and-eye closures around my back, and Santino has no problem freeing me from it and kissing his way from hip to hip and up my stomach. He plants kisses along the bottom lace trim of my bra and I inhale a sharp breath, squirming my torso away from his mouth.

Santino grins up at me. "Ticklish?"

"A little," I pant, and he runs his hands up over my hips, settling at the top of my ribcage so his fingers span my ribs and around my back, and his thumbs press into me right beneath my breasts.

"This was made for you, *farfalla*. You should buy it in every color. As a matter of fact, buy the whole damn store."

"It wasn't cheap," I goad, smirking down at him. I know exactly where Aria and Gia bought it.

"Good. I don't want you in anything cheap. I'll give you my credit card to buy whatever you want so long as it includes more of these."

"I'll see what I can do."

"But this set is special, Mrs. Antonucci. I want to see this on you every anniversary. And yes," he says, kissing me in the center of my chest, "I said *every* anniversary. Because I plan on being married to you until I take my last breath."

Santino keeps his eyes on mine when he leans in and places a kiss to each of my nipples that are hard and straining against the silk covering them. I sigh and pull my shoulders back, thrusting my chest forward, silently asking for more.

"Patience, my bride," he muses, the rumble of his deep voice against me sending vibrations straight to my already throbbing core. "Let me savor my gift."

Santino's fingers unhook my bra, slowly, one at a time, planting a kiss on one of my nipples every time he does, driving me insane and making my breasts ache and my pussy flood with desire.

There seems to be an endless number of hooks and I'm dizzy. His gaze and touch are hypnotic.

When he finally reaches the last hook, Santino runs a finger down my exposed spine and pulls his head back, bringing the silk fabric with him.

His eyes flare at seeing my exposed breasts for the first time, and my nipples tighten to the point of pain under his gaze.

"I need to taste you, *farfalla*. Please," he begs, cupping my breasts and filling his large hands with my sensitive flesh.

I choke on a moan. "Yes."

The moment his hot tongue touches my skin, I grip his biceps for support and my head falls back, a sigh of relief leaving me that turns into a moan when he squeezes my breasts and swirls his tongue around my taut nipple.

"Let me see your eyes," he demands, and I snap my chin down, meeting his eyes again. "I want to see your face and eyes for everything I do. I want to see what drives you crazy."

"This," I admit softly. "Everything. All of it."

Santino's blinding smile catches me off guard and I trace his lips with the tip of my finger. "Do you know how devastatingly good-looking you are? Devilishly handsome when you're all serious and unemotional, and roguishly sexy when you smile like this."

He catches my finger between his teeth and bites gently. I squeal and pull my finger free.

"I'm glad my wife finds me devilishly handsome and roguishly sexy. I'd be a little disappointed if she didn't like her view as much as I like mine."

I wish I had a witty response, but Santino's mouth is back on me, and all words and thoughts go right out of my head again.

He licks, sucks, and nibbles his way across my breasts, touching me everywhere but my stiff peaks.

"Santino," I growl in frustration, and he smirks.

"I want to make you come like this first, without me touching your pussy. Do you think you can?"

"I don't know," I admit honestly, albeit a little shyly.

"Well, I do, and you're going to come for me like this first. Just my mouth on your perfect tits to get that pussy nice and drenched for me to eat, okay?"

"Okay," I whisper.

"That's my girl." He winks and runs his thumb over one of my nipples. I cry out, the mix of pain and pleasure unexpected and amazing. "Give me your sounds, Mia. Don't hold back. It's just us here."

Santino swirls his tongue around and around one nipple, while running his thumb back and forth over the other. My legs tremble and my pussy throbs. He switches sides and repeats the torture, the sighs and moans leaving my lips foreign to my ears.

"Give in, Mrs. Antonucci," Santino demands in a gravelly voice that has me quivering all over. His lips latch around my nipple and he sucks me hard into his mouth while he pinches my other one, and I see stars.

My knees buckle and Santino pulls me against him to take my weight and keep me on my feet. I have no control over anything as my body breaks apart and falls at the feet of the man kneeling at mine.

My panties flood with the rush of my orgasm and Santino picks me up and carries me to the bed, placing me down on the end, right in the middle.

"You're so fucking sexy when you come, Mia. It's my greatest privilege to witness it and be the reason you do. I'm not done with you, either. I've been dreaming about seeing your pussy for the first time. I've already felt it squeeze my fingers as you came, so I know it's going to be perfect."

My God, he says the sweetest, dirtiest things, and I love it.

I lean back on my elbows and watch as he pulls my panties down. He brings them to his nose and inhales. "Fuck," he grunts, and shoves them in his pocket.

"Another souvenir? I thought you wanted me to wear this again?"

"I still want you to wear it again, just minus the panties. Then your pussy will be free to play with while I can look at the rest of you all dolled up."

Ohhh…

"You like the sound of that, my bride? I can see it in your eyes." Once again on his knees before me, Santino palms my knees and spreads my legs. "Fucking perfect. Just as I knew you'd be."

His gaze on my center has me leaking even more of my orgasm, and his nostrils flare.

"You smell divine, my blushing bride. Tell me I can have a taste. Tell me your wet pussy is mine to eat as the perfect dessert at the end of the most perfect fucking day."

"Yes," I breathe, feeling vulnerable so exposed to him.

Santino kisses his way up the inside of one thigh, and then the other. He's right there. His head is between my legs, his face a few inches from my weeping core, and he's looking at me like I really am a delicious dessert.

"I've never seen a more perfect pussy. I love that you have some hair for me, too. I can't wait to feel it on my face when it's buried in you."

Oh my God.

Santino presses my knees to the mattress and looks up at me, the devilish look in his eyes letting me know he's going to take everything from me before giving me an even more mind-blowing orgasm than the last.

"Keep your eyes on me as long as you can," he says, his breath warm on my wet core, making me shiver. "I want you to see me eating what's mine. I've never tasted a virgin pussy before."

That's oddly comforting. Almost satisfying, really.

I raise my chin haughtily. "Good. I deserve to have one of your firsts, too."

"You do," he agrees. "You deserve all my firsts, and I wish I could give them to you, but you should know everything with you feels new." He slides his hands down my inner thighs and back to my knees, leaving trails of goosebumps in their wake. "And trust me when I say you're going to get the most important first of all."

"Going to? Have you been married before?"

"No, my bride." He smirks. "You are my first and only wife, but that wasn't the most important first I was referring to."

"Then wha–" My question is cut off by his tongue sliding up my entire pussy, from my ass to my clit. "Ohmygod," I say in a rush. I've never felt anything so incredible. He swirls his tongue around my clit and my elbows almost give out, but I need to watch him longer. I need to cement the visual of Santino on his knees with his head between my legs in my mind so I never lose it.

I try to close my legs on instinct, but Santino grips the inside of my knees harder, refusing to let me. He drags his tongue back down to my entrance and rims it, then shoves his tongue inside me. I cry out, gripping the comforter on either side of me. I try, with all the strength I can muster, to stay up on my elbows, but it's too much. I collapse onto my back, already on the brink of exploding again.

"Santino," I moan, and he groans, spearing me with his tongue and pressing his entire face into my pussy. With my legs kept open, I have no choice but to let him take from me. "Santino," I moan again, and he grunts, bringing my legs around his shoulders and gripping my ass to keep me pressed to his face. "Yes!" I cry out, finally gaining some control. I squeeze my thighs around his head and grind my hips, practically fucking his face.

Santino flicks my clit with his tongue and sucks on it, pulling my hips further up off the bed.

I slide one hand through his hair and pull on the ends as he goes back to fucking me with his tongue.

"Oh my God. Oh my God. Oh my God," I chant as I'm pulled closer and closer to the edge. Santino doesn't let up. He's devouring me. He's eating me whole. He's consuming me like a starved man.

The new position has me looking up my body at him, and our eyes clash. The unfiltered hunger shining in his makes my chest tighten, then swell.

Keeping our eyes locked, Santino sucks on my opening, then he shoves his tongue in me as far as he can, and that's all it takes to push me over the edge.

I'm flying.

I'm floating.

I'm free-falling.

My back bows and my neck arches back, the throaty moan tearing through me chafing my already sore throat.

Santino doesn't let up. He draws out my orgasm, drinking my essence until I have nothing left to give.

"Please," I beg, tugging on his hair. "Please," I barely get out again before I give up and give in to the utter exhaustion of my mind and body.

CHAPTER 14
Santino

My wife is incredible. She's perfect. She was made for me.

Mia let me touch her. She let me kiss her soft skin. She let me tease her and play with her. She let me feast on her pussy and fuck her with my tongue until she creamed her sweet nectar right into my mouth. I've never tasted a better pussy and she's all mine, and only mine, for-fucking-ever.

She passed out from coming so hard and that satisfies me unlike anything I've ever accomplished in my life. I don't care how long it takes for her to trust me enough to let me inside her, because I know the day will come, and it'll be worth the wait. She's worth the wait.

I lift Mia up and carry her to what will be her side of the bed and tuck her in. She makes a little mewling sound that's a straight shot to my dick, and then sighs, curling into herself and remaining blissfully asleep.

I stare at her for another minute, admiring her innocence that's still written all over her, but is now forever tainted by me because my lips and face are still covered in her innocence.

Fuck, I need a cold shower.

I leave my shoes by Mia's on the carpet and quietly disappear into the bathroom. Closing the door behind me, I undress and toss my tux in the hamper, knowing my cleaning lady will sort it out for me when she comes.

I step under the spray of water before it warms up, needing the jolt to my system. Of course, it doesn't do anything to deflate my hard-on, and I wrap my hand around myself and close my eyes. I replay Mia at my mercy, the sounds she made when she was so far gone she couldn't control herself, the look in her eyes while she watched me pleasure her, and the look on her face as she came.

Fuck.

The head of my cock swells and I tighten my grip, bracing myself on the marble wall. I bow my head as the water beats down on my head and I pump my cock for some relief. It doesn't take long before the telltale fire licks down my spine and my balls grow heavy.

Knowing Mia is naked in my bed right now, I picture her begging me for my cock, and that's all it takes for me to blow my load.

Jesus, it's like I'm a damn teenager again. I haven't come this fast since the days when I could barely control myself. I'd be embarrassed if it weren't just me in here. Although, I have a feeling having Mia watch me masturbate, with those eyes that can get me do anything and are far too powerful for her own good, would have me coming just as quickly.

Fuck me, I'm adding that to my already long list of fantasies – us watching each other get off. I'd love to see Mia explore her sensual side and watch what she's only done in the privacy of her room.

I'm just going to get hard all over again if I keep thinking like this, so I quickly clean myself and then dry off. I wrap the towel around my waist and soundlessly walk across the room to the closet.

I would normally sleep naked, but I don't want to scare my new bride or have her think I'm pressuring her in any way, so I throw on a pair of flannel pajama pants, but not a shirt. I already don't like the feel of anything between me and my sheets, and I'm making an exception for Mia with the pants. Besides, she deserves a little preview of who she got as a husband.

I've always kept in shape and train regularly in kickboxing and Wushu to keep my mind and body sharp, agile, and ready for anything. I'm not oblivious to how it's all sculpted my body. I've had women lust after me and tell me how much they love my body, but it never mattered for longer than I needed to reel them in for the night, and then I never saw them again.

Mia, though…

I want her to look at me and *see me*. I want her to look at me with lust in her eyes, but I also want her to see past the exterior and lust after *me*.

I slide into bed and stare at my little butterfly. She looks at peace. She looks sweet and vulnerable. I'm sure she wouldn't want to sleep in her makeup, but I'm not waking her up. I don't want to break this moment in case it's all too good to be true and she'll wake up and regret everything. Marrying me, kissing me, saying yes to everything we just did. That'd fucking gut me. I'd rather her tell me no from the get go than regret anything we do.

I keep my eyes on her from my side of the bed even though the two feet between us feels like two miles, and all I want to do is pull her against me and use her heart beat as the steady metronome I need to help me sleep.

Instead, I stare at my wife's angelic face until my eyes close against my will.

CHAPTER 15
Mia

I wake to the morning light streaming in through the floor to ceiling windows and an empty other half of the bed. I know Santino slept in here with me though, based on the mussed sheets and blanket beside me.

I slept in the same bed with a man for the first time and I don't even remember it. I really hope I didn't do anything embarrassing like drool or snore or talk. I have no idea if I do any of those things on a nightly basis, and Aria and Gia have never said anything when I've stayed with them, but I still don't know.

Okay, relax, Mia.

I look under the blanket. Yup, still naked.

He tucked me in after all of…*that*.

I don't know what to do now. I've never felt anything as incredible as what I did last night, but what's the protocol for the next morning. How do I act?

I don't hear Santino in the room with me, so I quickly slip out of bed and dart into the bathroom, closing and locking the door behind me.

Oh, God.

What was I thinking last night?

I was caught up in the moment, that's what it was. It was the wedding.

I don't think clearly when I'm around Santino. He has a way of clouding my brain and my better judgement. Especially when he's saying all those sweet and dirty things to me, and making promises that sound so damn good.

I've never had a man touch me the way he did. Kiss me the way he did. The way he knew exactly what I would need. He gave me more pleasure than I knew I could experience.

And he's my husband.

I know how much he wants me, and if I wanted him to do that again, all I'd have to do is tease him a little bit and I'd have him begging on his knees again, but I shouldn't do that.

I shouldn't have let him to that to me last night as it is. Things went too far. Yeah, I got what I wanted from him, and made him see that he's the one who's going to be begging for what he wants, but this arrangement between us needs to be based on more than just our attraction to each other.

I can't even look at myself in the mirror right now. I walk straight into the shower and scrub my skin under the scalding water until I feel clean again. Until I feel like myself again. I don't know who this girl is that he's turning me into. I like her and I hate her at the same time.

I robotically grab a bottle of shampoo, but when the familiar scent hits my nose, I look at the bottle more closely. It's mine. It's my shampoo, my conditioner, and my body wash all lined up on a shelf in the shower.

What the hell?

How did he know?

My God, he's fucking crazy.

I look up at another shelf and see my facewash, too. I'm starting to think I married an insane person. Or a stalker of some kind. How else would he know?

I wash my face twice to make sure I get all my makeup off, and for a few minutes, I let the hot water beat down on me and let the steam envelope me until I realize I can't stay in here forever.

I turn off the water and grab two towels from the shelf beside the shower, wrapping my hair in one and my body in another.

Damn it, I don't have any clothes here. Just my wedding dress and lingerie, and fuck him if he thinks I'm putting either of those on again right now for him. I'll just have to borrow something of his.

I scurry across the room to his massive closet, and stop short when I spot my suitcase from the hotel sitting in the middle of the floor. Oh, right, he said my things would be here waiting for me. I reach for it and then stop short.

I look to the right and see that the entire side of the closet is filled with my clothes from back home in my apartment.

How the hell did he get them here?

Who did he have going through my things?

My shoes, purses, clothes, everything…

My jewelry, perfumes, and makeup. They're all here and organized in their own special places and on the small vanity in the corner.

This is all too much.

This visual.

His stuff on one side and mine on the other. It looks like we've been married for years.

It's overwhelming and I have no idea what I'm doing. The first thing I need to do is get dressed, and I don't want to set a precedent of dressing up for my husband like I'm some good little mob housewife, so instead, I put on a matching powder blue sweat set and a pair of my fuzzy slippers.

I go back into the bathroom, and of course, find all my haircare and skincare products in two of the drawers of the vanity. I detangle my hair first, and weave it into two French braids, and then go through my skincare routine before finally looking at myself in the mirror.

I'm the me I usually am most days. Simple, comfortable, and makeup free, and it brings me some semblance of comfort. Plus, I don't need the armor of a designer outfit and makeup to go and yell at my new husband.

What is he going to do, divorce me? Oh, what a tragedy that would be.

I leave the bedroom and the smell of fresh coffee hits my nose from down the hall, and I let my feet carry me towards it.

"Good morning, my beautiful bride," Santino says from his spot perched on a stool around the kitchen island. He puts his newspaper down and takes a sip from his coffee cup. "You look beautiful this morning," he tells me, his eyes trailing the length of my body and momentarily throwing me from my mission.

I stare at him, blinking, and then finally snap out of it. "How did you get all my things here? Why is my entire closet in your closet? Why do you have my shower products in your shower? My haircare? My skincare?"

"I had a few of my guys go to your apartment and pick it all up after you left for the hotel a couple days ago."

"And who gave you the right to let random men touch my things? You realize whatever men you sent had to touch my bras and underwear, right?" I place my hand on my hip and purse my lips in annoyance. "Did you think of that? That they got to see all my private things? While they were at it, I hope you told them to take my vibrator that was in my nightstand."

He smirks at that like the arrogant asshole he is and takes another sip of his coffee. "Do you really think you'll be needing that after last night? Has your vibrator ever gotten you off like that?"

"After last night, I'll most definitely be needing it, because last night isn't going to happen again. Last night was a mistake.

I shouldn't have let it get that far." Santino's expression completely changes from cocky to emotionless. It's like he's able to wipe his face of emotion in a single flip of a switch. I've seen Leo do it before and it's fucking creepy.

"Is that so? It was a mistake? It was a mistake to let your husband touch you?"

"Yes!" I yell, throwing my hands in the air. "You're only my husband because you forced me to marry you. So yes, it was a mistake to let you touch me. I must have had too much champagne to think clearly."

"You weren't drunk, Mia," he growls. "Don't you fucking dare try to use that as an excuse. Do you think I'd take advantage of you like that? That'd be assault, Mia. And you know what? You could've said no to marrying me," he counters, his voice low and controlled. "No one forced you. No one threatened you. It was an agreed upon arrangement."

"You weren't going to help my family unless I married you!" I remind him loudly. "How was I supposed to say no?"

"You have free will. Your family would have figured it out. They just chose the faster and simpler route – you marrying me."

"And now that I have, you seem to think you have this right to have me because you want me."

"You want me too," he says, standing quickly, and knocking his stool back in the process.

Santino stalks towards me, closing the distance in a few strides. I continue to back up to keep the distance, but I eventually collide with the couch in the connected living room.

He crowds me but doesn't touch me. "Don't make me out to be a monster, Mia. You want me just as much as I want you. I'm just the one who has no problem admitting it. I have no problem telling you how beautiful you are. I have no problem telling you how no other woman I've ever been with has made me feel even an ounce of what I do when I'm with you. I have no problem telling you that when I kiss you, it feels like the fucking world stands still, then spins out of control."

My heart is racing and I can't look away from his eyes.

"I have no problem telling you that I want to know every single fucking thing about you. I want to listen to you talk for hours about the things you love. About what you want to do in this world, where you want to go, what you want to see, who you want to be. I want to know everything. I'm completely obsessed with you, Mia, and I'm man enough to admit it to your face and to anyone who wants to know. I know you feel this craziness, too. I see it in your eyes. I see it in the way you react to me. You're probably scared, and I get that, but tell me that, then. Talk to me. Don't come out here after the best day and night of my life and start spouting shit about what a mistake last night was and how I'm a monster for forcing you into this."

I swallow hard, trying to keep from crying, screaming, or kissing him.

"Did I strategically get you to marry me? Yes, I did. Because I knew." He shakes his head and I straighten my spine.

"Knew what?" I ask, my voice hoarse from unshed tears.

Santino shakes his head and takes a step back. "I have

work to do. Make yourself at home," he says, spreading his arms out to gesture around the apartment. "I'll be down the hall at my brothers if you need anything."

I cross my arms over my chest indignantly. "I won't."

Santino stares at me for a beat, his emotionless mask still in place and his eyes completely shuttered from giving me any warmth like they did before.

Without another word, he grabs his wallet and keys from the counter and walks out of the apartment, leaving me frozen where I stand.

That didn't exactly go as planned. But to be fair, I already know I don't know what I'm doing. I don't know how to be a girlfriend. I don't know how to be a wife. I don't know how to be with a man.

I look around the apartment, and now that it's daylight, I can see how spacious, clean, and *nice* it is. I should've assumed as much, considering he's the head of one of the remaining four families in the city and it's a penthouse, but I always just assume men live like cavemen when they don't have a woman in their life.

And there's the problem. I don't know him. I married a man I don't know yesterday and I let him lick and kiss my body before eating my pussy like a starved man the same night.

Why did I do that?

I did that because despite not knowing intimate details of his life and all his likes and dislikes, he makes me feel alive. He makes me feel everything, all at once.

I could barely hold back from kissing him like a mad

woman just before, and I don't know what would've happened after that since I apparently have little to no control over my body and what it wants when Santino is near me.

Damn it, I need food. I can't deal with all this on an empty stomach and no caffeine.

Pulling myself together, I go back into the kitchen, and something on the island catches my eye. A note from Santino.

My beautiful wife,

Here's a set of keys to the apartment and one of my cars down in the garage, along with my credit card.

I have a surprise for you later if you're up for it.

Your new husband who's thankful his beautiful wife said yes to him last night,

Santino

A twinge of regret hits me in my stomach like a sucker punch, and I rub my forehead to keep an oncoming headache at bay.

Sighing, I pick up the keys and see a fob for a Porche attached to the ring. At least he's giving me a fun car to drive. Despite living in the city, my brothers made sure I learned to drive, which Santino obviously knows or he wouldn't have left me the keys.

I leave the note and keys on the counter for now and make myself scrambled eggs and toast for breakfast, with a side of the best cup of coffee I've ever had.

Damn, he buys the good stuff.

I spend the rest of the day rotting on the couch, watching a marathon of Vampire Diaries, wildly jealous of Elena. I would've chosen Damon, too. She's lucky she had a choice. I didn't get a choice. Or, maybe I did. I chose Santino in the club when I didn't know who he was, and I was willing to give him everything.

Damn it.

I don't know what to think anymore.

I turn the TV off and realize how hungry I am again. What time is it? I look at my phone and see it's already past six. And look at that, no texts or missed calls from anyone in my family.

Did I play my part as the blushing bride so well that everyone thinks I'm okay?

No one, not even Aria or Gia, thought to text me to see how my night was? If Santino tried anything with me? If I *let him* try anything with me?

I didn't expect my mother to check on me since we haven't spoken in over two weeks, but I am her only daughter. You'd think that would mean something considering I'm also the one who's taken care of her for years so no one knew how bad her depression truly got. I gave up my time for years without a second thought because she's my mom, and when I needed her, she decided I'm not important enough to fight for. She didn't even try to help me plan the wedding.

I would've taken anything from her.

Letting out a frustrated growl, I make myself an easy dinner of pasta with sauce that I added sauteed mushrooms, onions, and garlic to, and then watch a couple more episodes of Vampire Diaries before my eyes grow heavy and I sink down into a laying position on the couch.

Where's Santino?

He's been gone all day and now it's after ten and he's still not home.

He's avoiding me.

He's probably regretting marrying me after this morning.

I pinch my eyes closed and pray for sleep to finally take me so I can forget about everything for a few hours.

CHAPTER 16
Santino

"You know I love you, San, but why have you been hiding at my place all day instead of being home with your new wife? Don't you two have a lot of…"–Albie coughs–"talking to do?"

I level him with a stare.

"Alright," he says. "In all seriousness, why aren't you there with her? You married her yesterday and then abandoned her today."

"I didn't abandon her."

"Did something happen?"

"No," I grind out.

He grins like the asshole he is. "Sounds like it did."

"Shut up," I tell him, and he laughs.

"Shut up? What are you, a teenage girl?"

"Mia and I needed some space. That's it. Besides, we needed to go over everything for the meeting with the Melccionas tomorrow."

"Yeah, but we finished that this morning."

"Your point?"

"I think I've already made my point and I know you're not dumb."

Yeah, his point is that I'm hiding the truth from him and Emilio about Mia. They'd think I was crazy. Hell, I think I'm crazy. I saw her, wanted her, and found a way to have her.

Mia is a young, innocent, and beautiful woman with her whole life ahead of her to live. Except right now, she's down the hall, all alone with regrets fresh in her mind about tying herself to me and everything we did.

I'm hiding at my brother's right now like a pussy when Mia could've run away at any point today. I don't think she did, though. If she's going to run, then I know she'd want the assurance that she won't be chased. Because now that I've had a taste of her, no one else will do, and I'll chase her down no matter what.

I really am a crazy motherfucker, I guess.

"I'm out of here," I tell Albie.

"Finally," he sighs. "I'll see you in the morning. Go apologize for whatever you did or said that made you hide out here all day."

I flip him off as I'm leaving and hear his stupid laugh as

the door closes behind me.

Entering my apartment, I'm not sure what to expect, but it isn't Mia curled up on the couch, asleep with the TV on. I'd like to believe she tried staying up waiting for me, but that's just wishful thinking.

I turn the TV off and brush her soft hair away from her face and cup her cheek. She doesn't stir, so I slide my arms under her and lift her off the couch.

I lay her down gently on our bed, pull the covers over her, then strip down to my boxers and slide into my side of the bed, making sure I keep my distance again.

* * * *

I wake up at seven, a little later than my usual because I didn't set an alarm before I went to bed, and I shower and dress without waking Mia. I notice my note and the car keys I left for her yesterday on the counter are gone, and as my coffee brews, I write her another note, telling her I'll be gone until tonight. I doubt she'll wonder where I am, but I still want her to know.

We'll have to talk eventually, but I can't yet. I don't want to argue with her and I don't want to hear a repeat of anything I heard yesterday. I can't fucking do that again.

All the paperwork we need for the meeting is at Albie's from yesterday, so after my cup of coffee, I head over to his place and let myself in with my key.

"Hey," I greet, finding him in the kitchen.

"I could've sworn I locked my door last night," he says sarcastically.

"You did."

"You could've knocked like a normal person."

"I guess I'm not normal." I shrug.

"You're lucky I didn't have company over, cooking me breakfast while naked. I wouldn't want to tell your wife you're seeing naked women when you're not with her. Have you even gotten to see Mia naked yet? If not, think about how she'd feel if you saw a naked woman that wasn't her. She might hold out longer out of spite."

"Jesus, man." I rub my forehead. "Shut the fuck up and get ready. We're meeting Leo, Luca, and Nico soon."

"I'll bet she looks good naked." He smirks, knowing it'll piss me off. He's always loved finding any way possible to rile me up. "Not taking the bait? Alright," he sighs.

"Today is important, Alberto. We need to be serious. This was a part of the deal I made with Leo. We're finally getting rid of the cartel."

"I know this is serious, and I'm glad we're getting them off our backs and onto someone else's. Do you think the Melccionas will agree?"

"Luca said they took a hit recently, so they should leap at the chance. Plus, they were already in the drug game so they know how it works and have no inherent morality issue with it. They'll gain the upper hand again from the Jamaicans again and the other gangs around their territory. Now, go shower and get dressed and be out here in fifteen minutes, ready to leave."

"Sir, yes, sir." He salutes me and saunters off towards his room with his mug of coffee.

I pour a mug for myself while I wait, and by the time Albie emerges, Emilio has arrived.

"You didn't invite me to this little coffee date of yours. Should I be offended?"

"Yes," Albie says. "San clearly likes me more."

"I'm here because I knew you wouldn't be ready on time otherwise. I can count on Emilio to be early."

"Asshole," he grumbles, but knows I'm right.

We head down to the garage where our driver is waiting with one of our SUVs. I take the passenger seat while my brothers sit in the back.

When we arrive at the Carfano building, we're greeted in the lobby by one of their foot soldiers who takes us up to the third floor and into one of the larger conference rooms. I already noticed the additional men in the lobby, and I see the extras they have strategically placed in the surrounding conference rooms to look as if they're in meetings too.

All three men stand and shake our hands.

"Today will go exactly as we want," Leo tells us, the confidence in his voice leaving no room for an alternate outcome. It's why he's the head of the most powerful family in the city. He knows he'll get his way no matter what, and has every resource at his fingertips to ensure it happens.

He's gained my respect, and I trust him to hold up his end of our deal to get us out of the Gulf Cartel's business. Because if he doesn't, then he won't get my trucks, and without those, he won't be able to fulfill his contracts and will lose all respect and hierarchy position in our world.

If I was a vengeful man who loved my father, I would probably rejoice in the beginning of the Carfano downfall. But since I'm not, and I'm not looking to be the new target of every man and woman fighting for the top of the criminal pyramid, I'm choosing to help him. It benefits me far more than it doesn't. The main reason being Mia.

"How's Mia?" Nico asks, staring at me sternly.

"She's fine," is all I give him.

His jaw ticks. "That's it? She's fine?"

"You could always call her and ask her yourself if you don't believe me."

He takes a step forward to say something else, but Leo cuts him off. "Enough. We need to remain focused. We saw how fine Mia was at the wedding, and if she wasn't okay, she would have called one of us. You know that, Nico."

Nico nods and steps back to where he was.

"Besides, don't you recall how Luca's relationship with Angela started?" Leo adds with a little shake of his head.

"Oh, for fuck's sake," Luca mumbles, rubbing the back of his neck. "Don't compare the two."

"That's right." Leo nods. "Your situation was different. You kidnapped Angela and kept her locked away in your apartment until she fell in love with you."

"You kidnapped Cicariello's daughter and she ended up in love with you?" Albie asks incredulously.

"That's a simplification of it and not everything that happened," he growls defensively. "Don't make it seem like I forced her, Leo, or that she had Stockholm Syndrome or something. Jesus man, why did you have to drag me and Angela into this?"

"Because I had a point to make. You and Angela started the way you did and look where you are now. You never know with Santino and Mia. Give them time."

I don't know where this is coming from with Leo considering what he implied at the wedding, but I can only assume he was testing me or some shit, and now he can see that I don't mean harm to Mia.

One of Leo's men knocks on the glass door and opens it a fraction. "They're here, Boss. There's three of them and they're being checked for weapons now in the lobby."

"Thanks, Joey."

The man nods and goes back to his post beside the conference room door.

"Let's take our seats," Leo directs, and we all take seats that face the door so that when the Melccionas come in, they see us sitting as a united front.

A few minutes later, three men are escorted into the room by two of Leo's men.

"Good morning, Lou." Leo shakes their leader's hand first, then the other two, and I follow suit.

"Morning," Lou replies. "This is Sal and Frank." He says to me, pointing to the men beside him respectfully.

"Good to meet you."

Arranged

We take our seats and Leo takes control of the meeting from the start, going over everything we discussed as Lou listens intently.

"So, you want to just hand this over to us? We have our own trucks to do so, but why?" He directs the questions to me.

"My father made the deal when he was alive and I don't want to be involved with drugs anymore. I never did. We came to you because we know the Jamaicans are trying to gain a foothold in your territory and have been succeeding recently. This is a way to have a direct link to the source. I'm sure you can work out a deal with them for your own product to sell, but that part is on you to hammer out later with my contact, Javi. We're here to offer you that opportunity."

"And there's nothing in it for you?"

"There is," I tell him honestly. "I married Nico's sister on Saturday, so I'm doing business with them now. I don't have the time or inclination to continue my business dealings with the cartel. You and I both know pissing them off is not something one should do without expecting brutal retaliation, so we've chosen to find another transporter for them before moving on."

"You seem to know a lot about my business and what we're looking to do, Leo. You keeping tabs on your old uncle?"

Wait. Uncle?

Did he just say uncle?

"I have eyes and ears all over the city, Lou," Leo tells him. "You should know that. Just as I know you're a man who will take this deal seriously. Am I wrong in thinking that?"

"No, you're not."

"I didn't think so."

Lou looks to his men on either side of him, and the one to his right gives him a subtle nod. "If I agree," Lou starts, "then I'll need some assurances."

"Of course. We'll have a contract drawn up that we both agree on."

We spend the next half hour going over his terms and conditions, and I give mine, and we end up with an outline for an agreeable contract.

"My lawyer will draw this up and will send you a copy to review before we meet to sign. Then we can set up a meeting with Javi and have everything laid out for him so there's no delay in the transferring of hands."

"Sounds good. I'm glad we came. I wasn't sure what proposition you were going to lay out for me, but it's better than I could've hoped for."

"Good. I'll be in touch within the next day or two."

The three men leave the conference room with the same two men leading them out and down to the lobby again.

"That went just as you said it would."

"Did you not believe it would?" Leo asks, raising a brow.

"I did. It must be nice to get what you want all the time."

He smirks. "It is."

My brothers snicker and so do Nico and Luca.

"Did he say uncle?" I finally ask, not able to hold back any longer. I didn't want to look stupid in the meeting by asking in the middle of it.

"He did, but he's not my uncle. My mother's maiden name is Melcciona and Lou is her cousin. He likes to say he's my uncle to make it seem like he's somehow closer related to me than he is. I've never known him or thought of him as family, and don't plan on it in my lifetime."

"Interesting," is all I say, and Leo's eyes narrow.

"It's really not. Now, I want you to contact whoever you deal with from the Gulf Cartel and set up a meeting for the end of the week, preferably. We should have all the paperwork finalized by then."

I pull out my phone and scroll until I find the number I need. I put it on speaker phone so I don't have to relay the conversation afterwards, and it rings twice before the familiar raspy voice, thick with accent answers, "*Hola*, Santino. *Como estas?*"

"I'm good, Javi. You?"

"*Bueno, bueno.* What do you need?"

"We need to meet, Javi. This week, if that's possible for you. I have something I need to discuss with you that's important."

I have to be careful with how I word things. Javi can be a friendly man, but he's in charge of the shipments and transportation logistics in the Northeast for a reason.

"*Sí*, this week is good," he says. "Thursday night at the warehouse. Ten o'clock."

"That works. See you then."

I hang up and look to Leo who says, "I can have a surveillance team set up and waiting a few hours beforehand to ensure we're covered. I want this handled properly."

"You think I can't handle it properly?"

"I'm not saying you're incapable, Santino. I'm saying my family's business is relying on everything going according to plan. I need to have control over the situation so there aren't any ambushes. I take safety and planned precautions very seriously."

Of course he does. Especially after his father and uncle were gunned down on the street unexpectedly, and then with what happened at Giorgio's last year. "Fine, but a tip for you would be to not go at Javi aggressively or controlling like you're used to. He doesn't trust anyone. The fact that I asked to meet him about something important probably already has him thinking the worst and has his trigger finger twitching."

"Exactly," Leo says. "I am him. We'll get along just fine. You asked me for my help in getting rid of them from your life, so let me do that."

I scratch my chin and look out the windows for a brief moment. If I could punch Leo in the face, I'd relieve a lot of stress and pent-up aggravation I have right now.

My father, the bastard that he was, taught me to always keep a level head if I was going to be a leader and continue to have the respect of those around me. A hot-head can be feared for the unknown of what they'll do in any situation, but behind their back, their men don't respect them.

Fear and respect can go hand in hand if there's a balance.

I give Leo a curt nod. "As long as the deal gets done and we're all alive afterwards, we'll do things your way."

"Good." Leo claps his hands together and stands. "I'll get these papers to my lawyer and have them drawn up within 24 hours and sent to you and Lou. Then we'll discuss the plan for Thursday."

My brothers and I walk out of there, and it isn't until we're outside that any of us utters a word.

"He can be such an arrogant prick," Emilio says.

"Yes, but he has the right to be," I reply.

"You were rather accommodating, San," Albie comments. "You're letting him take control and making us seem like we can't handle our business or Javi on our own."

I whip my head around and pin him with a glare. "I'm doing what's needed to get out of the deal dad made. None of us want to be in business with the trigger-happy cartel who's known to have left a blood trail from here to Mexico from anyone who got in their way or looked at them wrong. The fact that we've managed to only lose 2 men since the start of this deal is a feat.

"I refuse to lose any more men or be brought down by them one day, and I know Javi won't simply let us off the hook if I ask him to. Leo is who he is for a reason. His reach is far and powerful. More than any of us. I'm man enough to admit that. If I need to step back and let him take control, then I will. And so will you and all our men. We'll be better off afterwards and won't lose any income in the process since we're now aligned with the Carfanos. Do either of you have anything else to bitch about, or can we get the fuck out of here? I'm starving."

"Jesus, man, okay." Albie holds up his hands in defeat. "I get your point. I just hate that we're the weaker ones in this scenario."

"I know," I agree, "but no one else will think that when we've successfully dissolved a contract with the Gulf Cartel and then partnered with the Carfanos."

"True. I get it."

"Me too," Emilio agrees, and it's good to know my brothers have my back.

We walk a couple blocks to grab lunch, and then I go back to Emilio's apartment for Monday night football. It's what we do every week during the season, but this week it has the added benefit of further avoiding talking to Mia.

I think a few days of space and time away from me is what she needs, anyhow.

CHAPTER 17
Santino

"*Hola*, Santino," Javier greets, coming out of the shadows in the warehouse beside the Red Hook Terminal. After the shipping containers come in to port, they're unloaded onto my trucks and brought here before transport.

"Good evening, Javier."

"So, why did we have to meet? Is there a problem?"

"No, no problem. I have a deal to offer you."

He tilts his head, skepticism written all over his face. "A deal?"

"Yes. I brought my new business partner with me to lay this out for you."

"Who?" he snaps, just as Leo walks through the door to join us. Javi reaches for his pistol, but I hold my hand up.

"This isn't an ambush, Javi. I just wanted to warn you before I introduced you two. Javier, this is Leo Carfano. Leo, this is Javier Cardenas."

"Leo Carfano," Javi says. "I've heard of you. It's impossible not to in this city."

Leo flashes him a wolfish grin that's anything but friendly. "Good to hear. Now, would you like to hear about our deal? We're both busy men who don't like to waste time with small talk, aren't we?"

"*Sí*, you're correct."

"Let's sit." Leo extends his arm to the office in the corner of the warehouse, and we all take a seat around the table.

Outside, are twenty armed men, waiting and ready to take out every cartel member present if Leo gives them his signal. He has men hiding in the rafters of the warehouse with rifles for just that purpose, and have been in place for hours.

Javi doesn't like to have a heavily manned security system method because he thinks it looks like he has something of importance in the warehouse and it will draw too much attention. Instead, he relies on cameras, which Leo's cousin, Stefano, was able to hack so the men could get in and in place without being detected.

One thing I can commend Leo for is his thoroughness when planning any type of meeting. He doesn't take anything for granted and risks no one's safety. He has all angles and scenarios covered in the event things go sideways, and I can honestly say I learned a few things from planning this meeting with him.

"Let me preface this meeting by saying that Santino has married into my family this past weekend," Leo states. "With that being said, we are in the process of merging our families and our respected businesses together. My family does not touch the drug business. We never have and we never will. So, Santino's connection to you was something I needed to take care of if him and I were going to move forward with our plans."

"Are you trying to fire me, Mr. Carfano?" Javi asks.

"Not at all. I am proposing to hand the transporting portion of your operation over to the Melcciona family. We've already met with them and they've agreed."

"And you expect me to trust some new family with my product because you say so? You've already revealed my operation to the Carfanos and the Melccionas, Santino. Do you think that was wise?" his voice takes on a deadly tone.

"My word is good, as you should already know," Leo tells him, ignoring the last statement directed towards me. "But to ease your doubts, I also have a signed agreement from them that mirrors your one with the Antonuccis. With an exception." Leo pulls out the envelope from his inner suit jacket pocket and hands it to Javier. "They've agreed to a five percent cut in what you're currently paying the Antonuccis for the same job."

"Well now, that's interesting."

"I thought it would be."

"Santino, what do you make of this deal? We've worked together for years. Leo says he doesn't like the drug business, but we've never had an issue. Money is money, is it not?"

"Like Leo said, I got married last weekend. She's a Carfano, and as such, we will now be merging our family businesses. I respect Leo's wishes to not touch the drug game, and it was my father who made the deal with you, not me. If you are willing, the Melccionas are available to meet with you whenever you are."

"And do they have an ulterior motive?"

"They want this deal. They know the drug business. The Jamaicans are encroaching on their territory and they need to get ahead again. They don't want to steal anything out from under you or push you out from selling in their area."

"Ah, so they have good motivation to remain loyal."

"They do."

"Alright, I agree to meet with them. We have a shipment that needs moving next week as you know, but I will not trust someone new on short notice to handle it. Alone, that is. If they pass the test, then I will meet with their boss."

"What test?" Leo asks.

"I want men from the Melcciano family to ride along with you to show them how it's done. If they handle it well, then we can talk. But," he emphasizes, holding up a finger, "if they get in the way, or it seems anything is going to go south, then you kill them, or I kill all of you. *Entiendes*?"

"Understood."

"*Bueno*. Then we'll talk again next week. I'll be here when you come to pick it up."

"You want me here to supervise?" I ask him.

"No, I want you in one of the trucks."

"I don't go on runs, Javi," I inform him coldly.

"But you have," he points out.

"That was years ago when I had to prove myself to my father."

His dark eyes are cold and calculating. "And now you have to prove yourself to me. I don't like change, Santino, and you've sprung a big change on me here. If you want me to trust the Melccionas, then you need to show me that you do."

I clench my jaw, keeping my temper from flaring. "If that's an assurance you need so this transfer can happen, then fine, I'll drive one of the trucks. However," I add, seeing Javi ready to speak, "this will be the only time and this will be the only test of trust you're going to get from me."

Javi cracks a grin that's anything but friendly. "I see marrying into the Carfano family has given you a reinforced set of balls and a shield to hide behind."

"I don't need anyone or anything to hide behind, Javier," I almost growl out, but hold back my anger. Fucking prick. If I could get away with putting a bullet between his eyes and not have to worry about the cartel hunting me down for revenge, then I would. But I'm not putting my family, or Mia, in danger like that.

Leo clears his throat and I know it's a message to get me to control myself.

I clench and unclench my fists under the table, needing a

way to release the anger building up in me.

I hate this.

I hate having to walk on eggshells around Javi so I don't piss him off and get killed. I hate playing second in command to Leo since he holds more power and respect in this city than I do. I hate that I have to go on a fucking run now when that's the last fucking thing I want to do. I'm the goddamn head of the family and I'm being made to do a foot soldier's job just to prove something to this asshole.

"If there's nothing else to discuss tonight," Leo says, "then we'll talk again after the shipments make it to their destinations." We all stand and shake hands. "Until next week."

Leo and I walk out of there and into our respective waiting SUVs, and I get a text from him straight away.

Leo: Tell your driver to head to Giorgio's and have your brothers meet us there.

Me: Okay.

I text my brothers and then sit back and close my eyes as Vince starts driving, my thoughts going straight to Mia. We're still not talking, and I don't know how to start again.

She hasn't left me any notes. She hasn't texted me. She hasn't uttered a single word to me.

To be fair, I've been coming home after she's already gone to sleep and leaving before she wakes up, but that's because I'm trying to be good. I'm trying to give her space. I'm trying to not push her too hard, too soon.

    At least, that's what I want to believe I'm doing.

CHAPTER 18
Mia

Santino has been avoiding me all week and I can't take it anymore. He needs to man the fuck up and stop avoiding me. I want to talk to him, but he seems to have a knack for leaving before I wake up and coming to bed after I've already gone to sleep.

Tonight, that all ends. I'm going to wait up for him and he's going to talk to me.

That's easier said than done, though, since it's past midnight and I'm exhausted from pacing the apartment all day, going over what I want to say to him.

I'm watching a movie in bed and my eyes fall closed

without me realizing it, then open again when Santino finally climbs into bed. I peek at the clock and see it's after two in the morning.

I turn over to face him. "You're avoiding me," I say, my voice groggy from sleep.

"You're awake?"

"I tried to wait up for you but I fell asleep. Now you're coming to bed in the middle of the night to avoid me?" I'm afraid to ask where he was or what he was doing this late.

"I had a meeting tonight. It went late."

"A meeting until two in the morning?"

"No. I went to eat with my brothers and your family afterward."

"Are you going to keep avoiding me?"

"Mia," he sighs, and I hate that he doesn't call me *farfalla*. I miss it. I miss him. I have no idea why, but I do. He's the one who wanted me so badly and made me believe I was important to him, and now he's backing off. He's gone all day, every day, leaving me alone in this stupid place that doesn't feel like home to me. Not that my other home felt like home to me, either.

"If you've changed your mind about me, and us, then tell me. We'll get an annulment and be done with it."

"Are you being serious right now or are you still sleepy and delusional?"

"I'm wide awake, Santino."

"Then listen carefully, Mia. I told you I was serious about you, us, and this marriage. I thought we had taken a step forward on our wedding night, but then you made your feelings clear the next morning. I've given you space and time without me. Is that not what you wanted?"

"You're such an asshole," I hiss out, and he laughs. He actually laughs.

"Now I'm an asshole for giving you space when you told me you regret everything we did? I was giving you time to sort out your feelings towards me, but you're still angry, so what should I surmise from that?"

"God, you're such an asshole!"

"You said that already."

I throw the covers off and storm out of the room. I need space from that insufferable man.

"Where are you going?" he asks, trailing behind me.

"Away from you!"

I hear him chuckle and I stop short, spinning around so fast, I almost lose my balance. "Don't laugh at me!"

Santino's smile is wiped from his face. "I'm not laughing at you. I just find this scenario a little funny. You didn't like me giving you space, but now you're running from me."

I ball my fists at my sides so tightly, I'm surprised my nails don't cut into my palms. "It's not funny," I growl.

He clears his throat. "You're right."

I throw my hands up in frustration and push at his chest, trying to shove him away from me, but he doesn't budge.

Instead, he covers my hands with his. "*Farfalla*," he murmurs, and I close my eyes at the sound of his name for me leaving his lips for the first time in almost five days. "Look at me." I open my eyes to see his are trying to urge me to understand him. "I don't want to fight with you. I don't want to stay away from you. I don't want our marriage annulled."

"I don't know how to do this and you need to have more patience with me," I tell him. "You know I've never been in any kind of relationship before. I don't know how to deal with everything I'm thinking and feeling. I loved everything that happened in the club, but I'm angry you tricked me. I'm angry that you manipulated me into marrying you, but then I realized you're not a bad man and I actually like you. Then I get angry at myself for enjoying any second I spend with you because of how we got to where we are." I shake my head, hoping he understands what I'm saying. "My head is a mess of contradictions, but my heart and body are quite clearly in agreement with what I want. I don't want to be angry anymore, though. I don't want to always be at war with myself, and I don't want to feel guilty for feeling and wanting what I do."

"Then don't. The only reason to feel guilty would be because you care what other people think or because we're doing something wrong." Santino takes my hands and places them around his neck. "And neither of those are true, right?"

I swallow hard, my mouth and throat bone dry. "I've spent my entire life having to care what people thought about me and my choices."

"Aren't you tired of living for everyone other than yourself?"

"Yes."

"Then what are you going to do to change that?"

"Are you goading me into kissing you?"

His eyebrows shoot up and his lips curl in a sexy little grin. "Is that what's on your mind? Because I'm all for it, *farfalla*. But if you kiss me, then it's a step you can't walk back. I can't hear you say you regret everything again and forever make me the bad guy in your eyes."

I don't even have to think about it.

I jump up and Santino catches me without hesitation. I wrap my legs around his waist and cup his face in my hands.

The stubble from his day-old beard scratches my palms in the sexiest way, and I trace his lips with my finger, memorizing them. He lets me take my time and doesn't say anything as I run my finger over his eyebrows and down his nose, then cup his cheek again.

"I'm going to kiss you, Santino," I whisper, not entirely sure why I'm warning him.

Leaning in, I keep my lips an inch away from his to prolong the moment. Santino tightens his hold on me and I smile, knowing he's trying his hardest to let me do this my way.

This moment feels big. It feels like everything.

My heart is pounding, my pussy is throbbing, and my entire body is shaking from the build-up of tension that has nowhere to go.

Finally, the rubber band holding me back snaps, and I crush my lips to Santino's. My hands slide to the back of his head and I kiss him until my head is spinning and my heart feels like it's going to find a new home outside of my body and inside Santino's.

I can't get close enough.

I clutch his head and squeeze my legs together, clinging to him like a lifeline.

He tastes like minty toothpaste, but behind that, is the faint taste of whiskey and cigars, and it's a lot more enticing than I thought it would be. He tastes like a man.

Tearing my lips away, I lean my forehead to his and squeeze my eyes shut. "If we don't stop now…" I trail off, shaking my head.

"It's okay, *farfalla*," he rasps, his voice rough and full of everything I'm feeling. "It's enough for me tonight. Trust me."

Santino walks us back to bed with me in his arms, and tucks me back in. When he joins me this time, he doesn't keep his distance. He slides to the middle of the bed and hooks his arm around my waist to pull me right up against him.

"No more space," he says gruffly. "It about killed me to keep my distance every time I came to bed."

I settle my head against his chest and come to realize he's not wearing a shirt. Was he not wearing a shirt this entire time and I was too angry and wound up to notice? Has he been sleeping next to me with no shirt on every night and I've been missing out on the view?

"I can feel you thinking," he says. "Just sleep, Mia."

I take a deep breath, inhaling his masculine scent, then release it slowly.

A few minutes go by, and I'm not sure if he's asleep or not, but I have to tell him the truth. The blanket of darkness gives me the little bit of strength I need to whisper, "I don't regret anything we did. I shouldn't have said that. I woke up and started freaking out, and then took it out on you because I could. I'm sorry."

Santino skims his fingers up and down my spine and kisses the side of my head. "Thank you," he whispers, the relief in his voice evident.

CHAPTER 19
Mia

I walk into the kitchen hoping to see Santino sitting at the counter, but there's a note instead.

My beautiful Mia,

I wish I didn't have to work today. I already know I won't be able to focus when I can't stop thinking about last night.

I've left you the name and number for a spa nearby. I've booked you in for the day, so choose whatever treatments you'd like.

My driver, Vince, will escort you to and from the spa, but then I'm taking you to dinner tonight and a surprise afterward, so be ready at 6:30, looking sexy. That shouldn't be hard for you at all, farfalla.

~ Santino

A spa day? How thoughtful of him. And he's taking me on a date tonight? Smiling, I clutch his note to my chest. Today is going to be a good day. The first I've had in what seems like a lifetime.

* * * *

I spent longer than I should have getting ready for dinner with Santino, but the butterflies in my stomach are telling me I'm just a girl who wants to look good for her husband.

My husband.

I'm going on my first date *with my husband*, and it's my first date ever. EVER.

After last night, there's no going back. Not that I want to, but now the butterflies of excitement are taking flight, leaving in their place a tangled knot of nerves.

I don't know how to date Santino. I don't know how to date anyone.

My breathing starts to become shallow and I grip the edge of the bathroom counter. But before it can become a full-blown panic attack, Santino appears in the doorway, freshly showered and dressed impeccably in a dark grey suit that's tailor-made for him.

He looks amazing, delectable, handsome, sexy.

He looks…like he's mine. All mine.

"*Farfalla*," he says seductively, the low timbre of his voice making that knot in my stomach loosen, "you're breathtakingly beautiful. Stunning."

I feel my cheeks heat under his awe-filled gaze, and it reminds me of how he looked at me while I was walking down the aisle – wanted, desired, and without a doubt, beautiful.

"Thank you," I say softly, letting my eyes travel over every inch of him. "You look really handsome."

His answering smile momentarily stuns me. This gorgeous man must have hit his head at some point to want me the way he does.

"Thank you, my bride," he purrs, and my insides completely melt and pool in my panties. "Are you ready to go?"

"I am."

He holds his hand out for me to take and I stare at it for a beat before slowly placing mine in his. He squeezes it and then laces our fingers together.

I grab my purse from the bed, but before we leave, he takes me into the kitchen where a huge bouquet of pink lilies are on display on the counter.

"Santino," I breathe. "They're gorgeous. Do they mean something too? Like the white ones?"

I touch their soft petals and Santino wraps his arm around

me to tell me, "Pink lilies represent grace, beauty, compassion, femininity, and admiration. You possess the first four, and I feel nothing but admiration towards you, *farfalla*."

"Santino," I whisper. "I love them. The spa day was wonderful too. Thank you."

Santino plants a soft kiss to the spot below my ear and then takes my hand again. "You're welcome, my bride. Now come, we have reservations."

As we're waiting for the elevator to arrive, Santino's brothers happen to show up and Albie whistles appreciatively. "Look, Emilio, the newlyweds are all dressed up. Date night?"

Santino's jaw flexes and I squeeze his hand, getting him to look down at me. I offer him a reassuring smile because I know his brother is just trying to get a rise out of him.

"Santino's taking me to dinner," I tell his brothers.

"How nice of him. And may I say, you look ravishing tonight, Mia."

"No, you may not say that," Santino growls. "Don't look at her."

Emilio and Albie laugh together. "Then maybe you should hide her away if you don't want anyone to look at your wife."

"Please don't give him ideas," I chime in. I wrap my free hand around Santino's forearm and he looks down at me again, his eyes softening immediately. "They're your brothers and they know what to say to set you off. Relax."

His shoulders drop and his eyes roam over my face. "Maybe I *should* hide you away," he says with a smirk, his eyes full of humor.

"You promised me dinner and a surprise, and I'm starving. You should know if I'm left hungry too long, I can't be held responsible for what I do or say."

Santino barks out a sexy laugh and swoops down to kiss my cheek, catching me by surprise. "Alright, let's go."

His brothers step back. "We'll take the next one," Emilio says when the elevator arrives.

"It's okay, you can ride down with us," I tell them, but Santino ushers me forward and punches the button for the garage level before Emilio or Albie can even try to join us.

"Thank you, Mia, but we'll wait. It was nice to see you again," Emilio says, and I smile at the two of them as the doors slide closed.

"Your brothers are nice. Funny, too."

"They're not," Santino says through gritted teeth.

"They are." I laugh. "And in case you have some weird thoughts on me wanting them in any way simply because I'm nice to them, then we should nip those in the bud right now."

"I know you don't want them."

"You do? Then why are you so tense around them and defensive?"

"Because they should be more respectful of my wife, that's why. I don't like them looking at you the way I do."

"To be fair, no one looks at me the way you do," I say without thinking, and Santino flashes me a wolfish grin, like I just gave him all the bait he needed before going in for the kill.

"Damn fucking right no one does." He backs me up until

my back hits the cool metal of the wall and lifts my chin with his finger while pressing his other to the spot against the wall beside my head. "I want to kiss you so damn badly, *farfalla*."

It's all I've thought about today, and honestly, I don't think I could get through dinner without kissing him again.

I give him a small nod in agreement.

The only place he's touching me is his finger under my chin as he presses his lips to mine in a kiss so soft, I almost feel like I'm dreaming he's kissing me at all. It's magical, but I need more, so I lift up onto my toes and kiss him harder, forcing him to give us both what we want.

Santino growls and kisses me back with a fierceness that has the air leaving my lungs and my legs ready to give out. Except before I know it, he tears his lips away and steps back, leaving me to sag against the wall.

He looks at me with eyes that have me knowing exactly what he's thinking, so I look at my feet, needing to gather myself again. I can hear his heavy breathing as he does the same, and when the elevator dings, signaling we've reached the garage, he grips me lightly above my elbow and walks us toward a sleek, gunmetal grey sports car, and opens the passenger door for me.

"Thank you," I whisper, maneuvering my way inside the low car in my tight dress without flashing him. He's already seen all of me, but I'm wearing a special lingerie set tonight that I know will drive him crazy once he sees it. I was feeling bold after the spa and picked it up on my way home, using the credit card he left me, of course.

The moment we pull out of the garage and onto the street, Santino places his hand on my thigh, and my mind can think of nothing but the searing heat of it through the fabric of my dress.

I went with a tight black dress that has a plunging v neckline and hugs my every curve. It's not short, and hits me right below my knee, but that doesn't mean I don't feel his touch right now as if he were touching my bare skin.

By the time we pull up to the restaurant and he removes his hand so he can give the keys to the valet and open my door for me, it feels as if I've lost a vital part of me without his touch. Like he's suddenly an extension of me, and without him touching me in some way, I feel a little…empty.

I think I'm going crazy.

I think I'm under some kind of hex or spell that has me suddenly needing this man like I need to breathe or function.

I could freak out – and I should be freaking out – about this and hide away somewhere in his apartment where we can continue to not speak or interact, but what would that get me? Hiding only delays the inevitable.

Santino places his hand on my lower back as we walk into the restaurant and I feel centered again.

Maybe dating my husband won't be such a bad thing. I just need to let go of what I think I should be feeling and instead just let myself feel.

I want to be here with him, and I like that his hand is on me to show everyone in here I'm his and I'm with him.

He makes me feel special.

He makes me feel wanted.

I've been on auto-pilot for so long, that the moment Santino pulled me into his arms in the club, it felt as if I were bolted awake by a strike of lightning.

I can't go back to how I was. I can't unknow what it's like to kiss him and have his hands, lips, and tongue all over me.

"Are you alright?" he asks in my ear as he pulls my chair out for me at our table.

"Yes. Just lost in my head a little."

"Good or bad?"

I smile. "Good."

"That's what I like to hear, my bride."

My bride.

He says it in such an old-fashioned way that it's endearing rather than condescending.

I sit down, and Santino helps me scoot forward before taking his seat across from me. Our server hands us menus and I thank him, and he gives me a little bow before walking away.

I look over the menu and tell Santino my choices, and when he orders for us, he takes on that commanding tone he has that gets me all hot and bothered.

I have the urge to run my fingers through his hair. I want to mess up the styling he did before mapping his every feature with my fingers as if I were a sculptor and needed to make sure I got every plane and line exactly right.

"What are you thinking right now, Mia?" he asks me when the server leaves, shaking me from my vision.

"That I want to touch you," I tell him honestly before I

second guess myself, and Santino's answering smoldering look tells me he would like that very much.

"You want to touch me," he echoes, his voice lowering to a sexy register that has my core pulsing.

"Your face, yes. And your hair. That's what I was thinking about while you ordered. Don't get too ahead of yourself."

"I wouldn't dream of it. Oh wait, yes, I would." He smirks.

I missed when he ordered a bottle of wine because of my little fantasy, and once my glass is poured, I'm grateful for the distraction and take a small sip.

"You do realize I'm not even 21 yet, right? That doesn't bother you?" I inquire, half joking.

"If it did, we wouldn't be sitting here right now. Does it bother you?"

"That you're older? No." I shake my head. "Of course, I've spent a while wondering why you'd want me when you could have anyone, but I have a feeling any girl who's with you would wonder that."

Santino's lips lift, fighting a grin, and I realize what I just admitted. "Mia," he says smoothly, "I don't care what any other woman feels but you. And to put your mind at ease, I haven't even looked at another woman since I saw you at Leo's wedding. And before that… Well, let's just say it's been a long time since any woman has captured my attention, and none ever have like you have."

"How many serious relationships have you been in?" I need to know. I need to know if he's given his heart to anyone, or more likely, how many hearts he's broken.

"One."

"Really? Just one? How old were you?"

"Thirty-four." He takes a sip of wine and I stare at him, puzzled.

"You're thirty-four now." He looks back at me without saying anything, and my brain finally catches up. "Oh, you mean me?" He nods. "But we're not really… We haven't been together long, or not *together*… I mean…" I shake my head and look away, not knowing where I was going with that.

"We're married, Mia," Santino says. "We're together. And yes, not for long, but you know I'm serious about you and us."

"And I'm the only one? That's hard to believe."

"Women have wanted me to be serious about them, but the feeling wasn't mutual."

"You know," I start, sitting up a little straighter, "I don't know if you think I should automatically feel flattered or thank you or what, but I'd be naive to believe the first man who pursues me is always telling me the truth or is the one for me. And if you've never been serious about any woman before me, how do I know I can trust you're serious now?"

"You think I'm lying to you?"

"I don't know."

"Let me start by saying that I'm not telling you things so you'll feel flattered. I'm just being honest with you. Everything I've said to you has been the truth, and it will continue to be. I don't believe in playing games. I don't have time for games. And as for me being the first man to pursue you, that's simply because every other man who's been interested was a coward."

I smile at that and take a sip of wine. I always did want a man who would be able to stand up to my brothers and not be intimidated or scared away by who they are.

How could I bring any normal guy into this world? He'd never fully be trusted by my family for them to include him in the business, and then he'd end up resenting them and me for something out of my control.

"Is that amusing?" Santino asks me.

"Not amusing, just an interesting choice of words."

"In what way?"

"I always told myself a man would be worthy of me if he could stand up to my brothers to be with me."

Santino's broad smile has my core clenching and my heart beating faster. He looks younger when he smiles like that. Like he has nothing in this world weighing him down.

"Your family doesn't scare me, *farfalla*."

"Oh, I believe you," I say on a laugh, "and I like that."

"I'm glad." If possible, his smile widens, stunning me. I think he knows what he's doing to me, too, because his eyes twinkle with a knowing gleam, and I'm glad he doesn't ask what else I like about him, because I'm not ready to admit anything else just yet.

Clearing my throat, I look down at my napkin in my lap. "Have you traveled much?" I ask, needing to steer the conversation into more neutral territory.

"Not as much as I'd like. My father saw no point in family vacations when there was work to be done, and my mother believed in her alone time and vacations and spa weekend trips by herself or with her friends."

I frown. "Oh, I'm sorry. That must have been disappointing."

"It was fine." He shrugs. "I always knew my mother didn't love my father and was only with him for his money and status. She had three kids just to appease him, and she got lucky by having three sons. Because my father had three sons to pass his legacy on to, he didn't care what my mother did with her time after we were a certain age. She gave him what he wanted and that was that."

"That's so… I'm sorry," I say lamely, not knowing the right words to convey how heartbreakingly sad that is. "You and your brothers shouldn't have had to feel like you were an obligation fulfilled rather than a gift to be loved and cherished."

Santino's eyes soften. "It's alright, *farfalla*. Thank you for saying that, but I had my brothers. We learned early on that we needed each other, and we were there for one another in every aspect that mattered. No matter what."

"I wish I had a sister for that reason. I'm close with my cousins, Aria and Gia, but it's not the same as having a sister. Plus, they're twins, so they already have a freakishly close bond that I will never be a part of. They're who took me to the club that night." I smirk. "They have connections all over the city through their modeling agency."

"I should send them a thank you gift."

"Why?"

"For taking you out that night." He places his hands on either side of his place setting and leans forward, telling me in a quieter voice, "And for giving me the chance to"–he pauses, lifting one side of his sexy mouth in a devilish smirk–"dance with you."

A nervous little laugh leaves me and I place my hand in front of my mouth to try to combat it.

"I love that sound," he says, his voice smooth and seductive.

"Then you should make me laugh more," I reply sassily, sitting up straighter and taking another sip of wine.

His smile returns, this time playful. "I'll try my best, my bride."

"Good." I lift my chin and study his eyes. "Because I can't be with someone lacking a sense of humor or that is without a fun bone in their body. I'd say you'd be a terrible husband for me then."

"Mia." He says my name in a low rumble that has my insides melting. "A day will never be dull or boring when we're together. And, baby, I'm the perfect husband for you. But if I'm ever being a terrible one, I have no doubt you'll tell me, just as I'd want you to."

I fight a smile. "I can do that."

"I know you can." He winks, and my insides melt further, making me think I'll be nothing but a puddle of mush for him by the time dinner is over.

We make it through our appetizers and entrees, talking about where I'd like to travel if I had the chance, our favorite songs and artists, and our favorite places around the city. By the time our server hands us dessert menus, I'm tipsy from the wine and drunk from listening to my husband talk about the things he loves and seeing his eyes light up every time I tell him something about myself he didn't know.

It turns out we both love Frank Sinatra, to which he promptly promised to take me dancing at a place he knows in Hoboken that's right on the water and has the best Sinatra impersonator and food.

We both love Chinese food at one in the morning because we think it's made fresher than during the day. We both have a love of early 2000s R&B and rap music. Him because he was the right age to listen to it when it came out, and me because my brothers and cousins always played it when I was growing up. We both love and hate New York City with the same passion. I've never met someone who felt the way I did, but we both also know we'd never want to live anywhere else.

He's promised to take me to all his favorite restaurants and I promised to take him to my favorite cafés. He even promised to go to my favorite museum with me so he could see what I find beautiful.

I am one hundred percent falling in love with my husband.

That thought hits me as I'm studying the dessert menu, and I breathe in a shaky, deep breath, hiding my face behind the menu for a moment.

"What looks good to you, *farfalla*? What's your favorite dessert?" Santino asks casually, but the sweet familiarity to the endearment, and his need to know my favorite of everything tonight, has me wanting to jump his fucking bones and beg him to take me home and have his way with me.

Instead of that, though, I say, "I think I'll get the tiramisu."

"Is that your favorite?"

"No." I smile. "My favorite dessert isn't anything I'll find on a restaurant menu." His brows furrow. "I love a double or triple scoop of cookies and cream ice cream in a waffle cone, smothered in rainbow sprinkles. But I also need an extra little dish of sprinkles on the side so I can continuously dip my cone in it after I've already licked them all off. Growing up, my dad would take me on special ice cream dates that were just him and I, and I guess I never outgrew it."

"Why should you?" He smiles. "I'd be willing to try your sprinkle method, but my favorite ice cream is mint chocolate chip."

"That's my second favorite flavor."

"Huh. Fate, it seems."

I roll my eyes playfully. "That your favorite ice cream is my second favorite? I'd hardly call that fate."

"Yes, because cookies and cream is *my* second favorite flavor. Our freezer will always be stocked with one we love and we'll both love the taste of each other's mouths when we kiss after we eat it." I gasp at his bluntness, then giggle. "Plus," he adds, lowering his voice, "I now need to know which flavor tastes better when licked off your body."

Oh, my God.

I feel my cheeks flush and Santino smirks. "Would you let

me do that one day, *farfalla?*"

I don't have any words, so I give him a small nod that has his dark eyes flaring with new heat.

He clears his throat when our server returns. "The tiramisu for my wife, and the ricotta cheesecake for me."

"Can I try yours?" I ask Santino when they arrive.

"Of course." He pushes his plate towards me and I do the same with mine.

I take a forkful of his cheesecake and a little moan escapes. "Mmm, this is so good. So creamy."

Santino's fork freezes on the plate while his eyes burn into mine. He doesn't look away for a long moment, and then he gives his head a little shake and finally tries my dessert.

Teasing him is fun. Especially when I don't even do it on purpose.

We finish our desserts and he pays, and when he places his hand on my lower back to guide me through the restaurant again, it feels more intimate than when we arrived.

I find myself wanting to be closer to him. I want him to put his arm around me. I want his hand to slide down to my ass and give it a little squeeze. I want him to brush my hair over my shoulder and kiss me below my ear before whispering how he's never been on a better date.

Outside, Santino hands the valet his ticket, and as we wait for his car, I shiver, prompting him to take his jacket off and drape it over my shoulders like they do in the movies.

"Such a gentleman, Mr. Antonucci," I tease.

"For you I am, Mrs. Antonucci."

"I'm a lucky girl, then." I smile, and his eyes widen, taking the compliment as it was intended. "This was the best first date I could've asked for. Thank you."

"Oh," he says, his face falling.

"What?"

"This was our first date, but this was also *your* first date. I should've made it more special. I should've flown you to Paris on a private jet and rented out the Eiffel Tower for a private dinner."

I can't help but laugh at his wild idea of a first date. "Santino, while that sounds *very* special indeed, not to mention incredibly expensive for a first date, it wasn't necessary. What made dinner so great wasn't the location or food. It was you. It was us talking and getting to know one another."

His cocky grin has me smiling right back at him. "Huh, well, isn't that fortunate?" Santino leans down and brushes his lips against my cheek and then whispers in my ear, "This was the best date of my life, Mia, but one day, I will take you on that incredibly expensive and so-called unnecessary date to Paris because *it is* necessary to me."

"If you insist."

"I do. But our date isn't over yet, *farfalla*. I still have that surprise I promised you."

I lean my face against his. "Show me, then."

CHAPTER 20
Mia

I don't follow where we're driving to because my attention is once again focused on Santino's hand on my thigh. My dress rode up when I slide into the car this time, and he pushes the fabric up an inch more so he can rub his fingers against my bare skin.

I'm lulled into a trance, and am disappointed when the drive ends and he leaves me feeling bereft again.

"We're here," he says, the rasp in his voice telling me he's just as effected as I am.

"And where is here?" I look out the window, but we seem to just be parked outside of someone's house.

"Our house," he says.

I whip my head back around to look at him. "Our house?"

"Yes, our house. I've owned it for a few years, and spent a year or so renovating it, but other than that, it's completely empty."

"But you have a place," I say lamely, which makes him smile.

"Yes, I do. I have a very nice penthouse apartment, but this is different. This is a home for us. Come, let me show you." Santino gets out and I keep my eyes trained on his as he rounds the front of the car and opens my door for me. I take his hand and look up at the beautiful brownstone from the sidewalk.

We walk up the steps and I look up and down the block as he fishes his keys from his pocket and opens the door.

An alarm goes off, and he promptly punches a code into the box on the wall beside the door. "A security update was one of the major things I had done. There are cameras covering every inch of the outside, sensors on all the windows, and a panic button hidden in the bedroom in case something happens in the middle of the night that alerts 911."

"It sounds…" I search for the right word. "Safe?"

"I always want you to feel safe, even when I'm not around. Especially then. It will give me piece of mind, too, knowing you're safe."

I look around the empty living room and immediately see visions of what I'd put in here to make it look homey while working with the natural architecture and features to keep its charm. The floors are hardwood, the fireplace is framed by a vintage French-styled mantel showpiece, and the front window is rounded out and perfect for a seat beneath it. The staircase leading to the second floor is gorgeous with its hardwood paneling up the side, and my jaw drops when Santino leads me down the hall to the kitchen.

"Santino," I whisper. "This kitchen is beautiful. It's a dream, really. Did you pick everything out yourself?"

"I did."

I smile at him. "You did a good job, Mr. Antonucci. I'm impressed."

"Thank you, Mrs. Antonucci. This whole house is yours to do with what you'd like. Fill it with everything you want, change whatever you don't like. I won't be offended. Trust me." He grins. "I want you to be comfortable and feel at home here. My apartment is yours as much as it's mine, of course, but this will be all ours from the beginning."

"Santino," I breathe his name, stunned by the gesture. "This is a pretty big surprise." He's letting me make my own home.

"I suppose."

"You know, giving me free rein on fully decorating and furnishing a house like this will force me to spend a lot of your money, right?" I giggle and cover my mouth, loving the look on his face. He looks equally pleased and nervous. "Don't worry, husband, I won't bankrupt you."

"You couldn't even if you tried, my wife." Grabbing my hand, Santino spins me around and pulls me flush against him.

"So, you like your surprise?"

"I love it," I whisper. "Thank you."

"You're welcome," he whispers, my eyes on his lips. "I've always wanted to own a brownstone, so I bought this one when the price was right, but I had no reason to live in it by myself. Especially when I could live down the hall from my brothers. But now…"

"Now?"

"Now, all I can picture is coming home to you here."

"That sounds nice," I say softly. "I can picture a lot of things with you in here."

"You can?"

"Yes. Maybe because tonight has been so incredible, but I think I–" I cut myself off, seeing his eyes flare with a fierce desire. I almost just told him I was falling in love with him.

"You think you, what?" he prompts, urging me to continue.

"I think I," I repeat, my voice barely above a whisper, afraid to say it out loud. In fact, I can't say it out loud at all, but I can show him.

I throw my arms around his neck and bring his lips to mine in a crushing kiss that changes everything between us.

I initiated it.

I didn't beg and he didn't beg.

I'm kissing him because I wholeheartedly *need* to. I need to feel his desire like my own and give him something I can't put into words just yet.

I kiss Santino like I'll never get another chance, and he

gives me everything I already know he feels for me in return. He lets me feel his desire, his need, and his obsession, and I return it with just as much fevered passion.

Santino wraps his arms around my back and his jacket slips from my shoulders and pools at my feet. I run my fingers up the back of his head and mess up his perfect hair the way I envisioned during dinner. I grip thick chunks in my fists and he groans into my mouth. The vibrations travel through me and stoke the fire already blazing through my veins, turning me into a completely savage being who can only think of one thing – *more*. More of everything.

I scratch at his scalp and he grunts, sliding his hands down to grip my ass. I groan, and he uses the opportunity to slip his tongue into my mouth and taste me fully.

I press myself as close as I can to him, but it's not enough. I need to be closer.

His cock is hard against my stomach, so I try to move against him to tell him I need more, and he grips my ass tighter, making me moan into his mouth and bite down on his lip.

"*Farfalla*," he growls.

Santino slides his hands below my ass and lifts me up and spins me around in a swift motion that has me dizzy. He plops me down on the kitchen island and growls in frustration when he can't easily spread my legs to step between them because of my dress.

"This dress is so damn tight," he chastises, and the animalistic roughness to his voice makes my insides pool between my thighs.

"I didn't think you'd complain about that," I say breathlessly.

"It's keeping me from my heaven, baby. Come here." Santino tosses me over his shoulder like a rag doll and grips the hem of my dress below my knees and lifts it above my ass in a single motion before sitting me back down on the counter.

Holy shit, that was hot.

He spreads my legs apart and steps between them, pulling me forward until my core meets his hard length. "That's better," he praises, and my head falls back with a moan. "Fuck," he grunts. "You're so fucking beautiful, Mia. My dream come true."

Santino's lips travel the length of my neck up to my jaw, and he kisses his way over to my lips.

"Santino," I sigh, slicing my fingers through his hair.

"Where do you want my attention most, Mia? Here?" He kisses my lips and glides his hot tongue across my bottom lip. I nod yes, but then shake my head no. "Here?" His hands slide up my waist and he cups my breasts through my dress, squeezing my aching mounds. And while it feels incredible, I shake my head no again. "No? Then where, my bride? Where do you need me most?" His hands slide back down my sides, down the length of my outer thighs, and then back to my waist. "Here?" He rolls his hips so I feel his hard length hit me right where I need him most, and moan, nodding my head frantically.

"Yes," I breathe, my vision blurry with desire as I look into his dark eyes that are like two bottomless pools of dark chocolate I'd love to dive right into and drink from like a savage.

"You want my fingers or my mouth there, *farfalla*?"

I shake my head and his eyes turn even darker, if that's possible. "There's only one other option, Mia."

He uses my given name when he's serious, so I blink to clear my vision, wanting him to see my clear choice.

"Yes, I know." I drop my hands to the tops of his shoulders and around to the buttons on his shirt, undoing one. "I want to see you, Santino. I want to see my husband." His chest rises and falls with heavier labored breaths, and I can feel his heart pounding as I undo another button. "It's only fair since you've seen all of me. Don't you think?"

Apparently, I've rendered him speechless, because he only manages to nod his head.

"And the deep ache I feel inside me won't be reached by your fingers or your tongue, Santino."

"Mia," he chokes out, my name a desperate plea.

"Just show me my husband first. Let me see what's mine."

"I'm yours," he says fiercely as I undo another button, like he didn't believe the statement until I said it. "And if you want to see what's yours, baby, I'll happily oblige."

I continue to unbutton his shirt as he kicks off his shoes, undoes his pants, and steps out of them. I get to the last button and then boldly place my hands inside the parted fabric, flat against his chest. My breath hitches on contact while he hisses.

"Fuck, Mia, just your hands on me like that feels so good."

I can feel his heart pounding a steady rhythm that aligns

with the throbbing of my core. I know he'll take care of me soon, so this is my time to admire him and give him just a piece of the appreciation he's shown me.

I rake my nails down his chest and he shivers under my touch, hissing out another short breath that turns into a dark chuckle.

"I didn't realize you'd have a little sadistic side, *farfalla*. But that evil little satisfied grin you're wearing tells me there's so much to explore with you that you don't even know is possible yet."

"Good thing I have you to show me." I slide my hands up and over his shoulders, pushing his shirt off.

"I'll show you anything you desire, Mia. Anything. Whenever you want."

Leaning forward, I plant a kiss in the center of his chest, the desire to feel his skin on my lips too great to ignore any longer. "I know."

"Good," he says, his voice strained.

I lean back on my hands to admire him. From his disheveled hair, down to his hips between my thighs, and back up. I take in every inch of his solid frame, and when I hold my hands up to touch his forearms, I look into his blazing eyes and wait for his small nod of approval before touching him.

I skim my fingers up both of his arms, feeling his muscles bunch and release as I pass over them. He's so strong. No wonder he was able to lift me over his shoulder just before like I weighed nothing at all.

I swirl my fingers on top of his shoulders and smile when

he twitches as I go down his back as far as I can reach before coming back up and over his shoulders and down his chest and abdomen. His stomach muscles tense and twitch as I skim over them, and I can't wait to feel them do that against my mouth as I kiss my way around his body.

I rake my nails over his ribcage and down across his hips, loving the tense set to Santino's jaw. I know it's taking everything in him to hold back and let me remain in control.

When I run my finger along the waistband of his sexy black boxer briefs, Santino presses his palms onto the marble countertop on either side of me.

"Mia," he rasps, "I don't think I can take you teasing me for much longer. Your hands on me have my cock so fucking hard, I'm having trouble seeing straight, let alone have a clear thought in my head that isn't me begging you to wrap your delicate hand around my throbbing cock and making me come all over your soft thighs."

I hook my finger under the elastic waistband and snap it against his taut lower stomach. "You don't have to beg tonight, Santino," I tell him, running my other hand up and down his thick forearm. "I want to touch you so badly. I just want to make sure you enjoy it."

He presses his forehead to mine. "Trust me when I say that you touching me is enough, baby. Whatever you do. But I'll guide you if you'd like."

"Yes. Please."

"Slide your hand into my boxers, *farfalla*." The deep, gravel tone of his voice has me ready to do whatever he tells me to. I reach into his boxers and grip his cock, loving the hot, hard, and heavy feel of him in my hand. "Yes," he groans. "Now squeeze a little." I do as he says and he groans again. "A little harder, baby. Now slide your hand down to my tip. Use the cum that's already leaking out of me as lubricant."

I follow his directions as he gives them to me, and with how he reacts to my touch, I feel powerful. I have power over this powerful man. A man who did whatever he needed to in order to make me his, and now that I am, I see how much power I hold over my dear husband.

Feeling confident, I take control and glide my hand up and down his length, squeezing him just a little tighter each time.

"Fuck," he grunts. "I'm almost there, Mia. Just—" he chokes, cutting himself off.

"I want to feel you come, Santino. Give me my reward."

"Fuck," he grunts again, and I grin, tilting my face up to capture his lips in a hot, wet kiss, as I pick up the pace and rub my thumb over the tip of his cock on each pass.

"Mia, Mia, Mia," he chants.

Santino bites down on my lower lip and then groans long and low into my mouth as hot cum coats my hand.

"Fuck, you're perfect," he says when he catches his breath.

"Far from it," I tell him. "But I'm glad you think so."

Santino slams his lips against mine and demands entrance with his tongue right away, entangling his with mine in a way that's possessive, claiming, and appreciative all wrapped together.

I wipe my hand against his boxers as I remove it and wrap my arms around his back, pulling him back against me. I rock against him, feeling his cock quickly grow hard against me again.

"*Farfalla.*" Santino grips my hips to halt my movements. "Is your pussy throbbing for me? Did making me come turn you on?"

"Yes," I hiss, trying to move again, but he grips me harder to keep me still. "Santino," I whine, "I ache even more now. I need you. I want you. Please."

"Are you begging me for my cock, *farfalla*?" He pulls back to look into my eyes and mine widen when I realize he's right. "It's okay, my beautiful bride, I won't hold it against you, nor will I make you repeat yourself so I can hear how sexy you sound when you're begging for my cock. I will say that this moment is even more perfect than I envisioned in my head."

I give him the best withering glare I can muster while in my frantic state, but he just smirks, the cocky bastard.

"I'm not going to give you my cock, *farfalla*. Not here."

"Wh-what? Why not?" I question, nervous I ruined the moment.

"Your first time needs to be special. It needs to be in a bed, with you laid out beautifully and me worshipping every inch of your body until you're ready for me. Then, I'll be gentle with you. I'll let you get used to me and my size and make slow love to you." My breath hitches. Make love? "After the first time, though, I can't guarantee I'll be gentle again, though, because every time I see you and am near you, I have the inexplicable need to rip your clothes off and fuck you until you're screaming my name."

"Santino," I whisper, digging my nails into his back.

"Yes, baby, but much, much louder."

"Then maybe you should take me back to your apartment where you have a very nice, big bed, and you can do all of that."

Santino kisses me hard and fast, then lifts me off the counter and sets me back on the floor where he pulls my dress down for me and quickly puts his clothes back on.

He takes my hand and walks us out of there, only remembering at the last second to turn the lights off and set the alarm before closing and locking the door behind us.

I almost giggle at the notion that he's too distracted by me to think straight, but I don't. I like the idea too much.

CHAPTER 21
Santino

Mia is perfect.

She was made for me.

I already knew she was, but with every second I spend with her, it's solidified.

I drive us home as fast as I possibly can in this city, running through everything I'm going to do with her when we get there.

Mia wants me.

She told me she wants me. She told me she needs me.

She fucking begged for my cock.

If she hadn't already just made me come, I would've from

her words alone.

I think Mia is starting to know her power over me, and it's going to be fun seeing what she can get me to do once she knows how to fully wield that power over me.

I keep my hand on her thigh and squeeze, needing to get her naked five minutes ago.

If it wasn't her first time, I would've fucked her in our new kitchen and christened the damn place the way it should be. But I can't do that to her. Mia deserves the gentleman I want to be for her. She deserves the most unselfish version of me her first time.

The moment I park in the garage, I hop out and jog around to open her door. She takes my hand and looks up at me with a smile that has my dick throbbing painfully and my heart beating out of sync like she just reached inside my chest and wrapped her hand around it.

"Why are you looking at me like that?" she asks, the sweet melody of her voice like music to my ears.

"How am I looking at you?"

"Like you can't wait to be upstairs with me." She smiles sweetly and my vision blurs for a second before clearing again on her angelic face.

"Well, that's exactly how I feel, and I don't need to hide that from you."

"No, you don't. Let's go." She squeezes my hand and I tug her forward, kissing her until I feel her slump against me, unable to hold herself up any longer.

"Santino," she sighs, and I scoop her up into my arms and

carry her to the elevator where she giggles and bites her lip. "I can walk."

"I don't know. You seemed to be pretty lax in my arms just a moment ago. I didn't want to risk you twisting your ankle in those sexy heels of yours having you walk on your own."

"Good thinking. A trip to the doctor might kill the mood."

I don't tell her, but it wouldn't kill the mood for me. I'd still want to fuck her until she passes out no matter what. I'd just be more careful with which positions I took her in.

"Then I'm not putting you down."

"Okay," she says softly, her cheeks turning pink.

Jesus Christ, she's adorable when she gets shy.

I want to see her turn pink all over when I get her naked and spread open on our bed.

In our apartment, I walk us straight to our room and place her on her feet at the end of the bed.

"I'm going to undress you, Mia," I tell her, and she bites her lip and nods.

I bend down and grab the hem of her dress, peeling the skin-tight fabric up and off her body to reveal a sexy lingerie set of black silk panties and bra that barely cover her.

"Mia, you're stunning." I have no other words. She's the most beautiful woman I've ever seen. "Are you sure about this? I can still walk out of this room, pour myself a large glass of whiskey, and sleep on the couch."

"I don't want you to leave. Tonight was amazing and I want you to keep making it amazing. I want you to keep making me feel good. I want you to keep making me feel special. I don't want tonight to end. I want you to show me how much you want me, Santino."

I tuck her hair behind her ear and run the backs of my fingers down her neck to her exposed shoulder. "I can do that, Mia. It will be my greatest honor."

Mia smiles. "Sometimes you say the sweetest things."

"Only for you, my bride." I tilt her chin up and plant a soft kiss to her lips, feeling her relax and melt against me like she did before. It's a feeling I've never felt before, knowing I can make Mia melt with a simple kiss.

I unclasp her bra and pull it form her body, replacing the satin with my hands. She moans and throws her hands around my neck, kissing me with a passion I hope I never get used to.

I knead her breasts and roll her taut nipples between my thumb and forefingers. Mia chokes on a moan and I swallow it as my prize. I want all her sounds. I want all her cries of pleasure and her pleads for more.

She's all mine to take, and I'm going to make sure she remembers it for the rest of her life without a single regret.

She pushes my jacket off my shoulders and starts to undo the buttons of my shirt. It's not nearly fast enough, so I push her hands away and rip the goddamn shirt open.

"That was hot," she croaks, and I laugh.

"I'll remember that."

"Please do."

"Lay back, *farfalla*. Let me see you laid out for me to worship."

She does as I say so beautifully, and I finish shedding my clothes before placing one knee on the bed to join her.

"Wait," she says, holding her hand up. My heart jumps into my throat. "Let me look at you for a moment. Stand back up," she directs, and my body relaxes, realizing her intention.

I stand at the end of the bed and she props herself up on her elbows. The heat of her eyes traveling around my body has my cock stiffening painfully.

"Turn," she demands softly, but with clear authority.

I don't mind feeling like a piece of meat. I want her to look at me, ogle me, and objectify me all she fucking wants. I'm her goddamn husband and all hers to do whatever she wants with.

I turn in a slow circle, and when I'm facing her again, she's wearing a sly little grin that's sexy as hell.

"Very nice, husband."

"I'm glad you think so, wife."

"Now, please," she says, running her hands up her stomach and over her breasts, "I want you to do everything you promised."

Fuck. Me.

"I'm a man of my word, *farfalla*."

Starting at her ankles, I kiss my way up each of her legs, loving the way she squirms and the way her breath catches every time my lips make contact with her skin. She's so responsive.

At the apex of her thighs, I run my nose up the seam of her silk-covered pussy, and suck her through the fabric.

"Santino!" she cries out, grabbing my hair in her fist.

I bite the top of her panties and lift her hips off the bed to drag them down her legs.

"Do you plan on keeping those, too?" Mia asks, her eyes alight with humor.

"I do." She rolls her eyes and I pry her legs open in a quick motion, pressing her knees to the mattress. She gasps and I smirk. "Don't roll your eyes at me, *farfalla*. I need mementos from our wedding night and tonight. Two memorable nights."

"Oh," she says, her pouty lips forming the perfect little O that has my mind conjuring images of her lips stretched around my cock as she takes me deep into her hot little mouth. That's for another time, though. Tonight is all about her.

"Yes, baby. *Oh*. Now, let me feast. I'm going to make you come at least twice before I fill you with my cock." Her eyes glaze over with lust. "I want to make sure you're soaking wet and ready for me. Sound good, my bride?"

"Yes," she sighs, lifting her hips as an invitation.

Kissing my way up her torso, I swirl my tongue around her bellybutton and she grips my hair again, loving her need to connect to me. I lick the rounded paths under her perfect tits. They're just the right size, *and real*. I could spend hours licking, kissing, and suckling on her sensitive flesh, and listen to sexy moans and sighs like the beautiful music they are.

Mia squirms beneath me and hooks her legs around my hips so I can feel how wet she already is.

I finally give some attention to her perfect nipples and she moans loudly, rolling her hips against me.

"Yes," she sighs, panting. "More, please," she begs, and I suck on her nipple with enough force that she cries out, bucking her hips against me. "Santino!"

"That's one," I rasp, loving that I can make her come just by playing with her tits. So sensitive. So responsive. So willing to give herself over to me to take care of her. So beautiful.

I slide my hand down between us and coat my fingers in her sweet cream before dragging them up her body and circling her nipples. I follow the trail I left back down her body, humming my approval as I go.

Holding Mia's legs apart, I look up at her from her hips and commit to memory the beautiful sight before me. Her skin is flushed from her first orgasm, her chest rises and falls quickly with her short breaths, her hair is splayed out around her like a halo of light, and her angelic face is the picture of pleasure. Her head is tilted back, her eyes are pinched closed, her mouth slightly ajar, and her cheeks a bright flushed red.

I'm the luckiest man in the fucking world.

I run my middle finger down her center and rim her entrance, and my eyes leave her face to see her pussy leaking cum.

She wanted to fight me, and this, and deny herself what I already knew was going to be amazing, but her body's reaction and response to me is all the validation need. It can't be faked.

I need to taste her again. I've been desperate for more of her, and now I get to have all of her.

I lick her from her tight little asshole to her clit, and Mia's hips buck up off the bed with a shout. I press her back into the mattress. I can't have her taking control and riding my face just yet.

I eat her pussy until she's shaking, gripping the sheets with white knuckles, and her mouth is open in a silent scream.

I have her right on the edge.

Shoving two fingers deep inside her, I suck on her clit and she explodes. Her pussy squeezes my fingers and pulses around them, seeking more. And fuck me, I can't wait to feel her do that around my cock.

She's as ready as she'll ever be, so I crawl up her body and kiss my way up her neck, across her jaw, and over to her lips so she can taste herself on my tongue.

"Santino," she sighs, the sound a direct shot to my chest, all breathy and satisfied.

"Mia," I murmur against her lips between kisses.

I pull her knees up beside my hips and align myself at her entrance, using all my willpower not to thrust forward and be inside her in an instant.

She tenses just the slightest. "Don't worry, *farfalla*, I told you I'll go slow."

CHAPTER 22
Mia

I'm about to lose my virginity.

I'm about to lose my virginity to my husband.

My husband who arranged our marriage so he could have me.

I couldn't care less about that. I don't care how we got to this moment, because this moment is everything, and I one hundred percent am glad it's Santino I'm doing this with.

"Wait," I say in a panic, and his eyes flash with what I think is pain. "Condom," is all I manage to get out, and the pain turns to understanding.

"Sorry, baby, I got lost in you." He reaches into the drawer of his nightstand and pulls one out. Sitting back on his heels, he rips the packet open, and I watch him roll it down his impressive length. He looks even bigger than before.

How…

How is he going to fit inside me?

"If you keep looking at my dick like that, Mia, this isn't going to go the way I want it to."

I bite my lip and raise my eyes to his. "Sorry."

He groans and runs his hand through his hair. "Don't be, baby. You looking at me like that is the greatest fucking thing. I love it."

I reach for his hands and pull him back down for a kiss. I can still taste myself on his lips and tongue and it's oddly erotic.

"Make love to me now, Santino," I whisper against his lips, feeling him at my entrance again.

He made me come twice already, but my body needs more. I need more. I want to feel him inside me, stretching me, filling me, and reaching that deep ache that he hasn't yet.

"Your wish is my command, my bride."

Santino keeps his eyes on mine, looking so intensely, it's like he's trying to reach my soul as the fat tip of his cock presses into me.

I'm already beyond wet, so he slips in easily, but I tense up, the intensity of his size already making me panic.

"Relax, Mia. It'll only hurt for a moment, and then I promise it'll feel good. So fucking good, baby. Do you trust me?"

He searches my eyes for the truth, and I let him see that I

do. "I trust you."

"Then breathe for me, *farfalla*. I'm going to push in a little more and it'll hurt less if you relax and breathe."

I nod my head, but I don't know how I can possibly follow any sort of directions right now.

He reaches between us and rubs my clit, instantly making me feel fire lick across every inch of my body, and I automatically lift my hips to take him inside me just a little bit more.

Ohhh.

My breathing becomes erratic and my eyes widen as I feel him stretching me painfully.

"It's too much," I pant.

"You were made to take me, Mia. Your body will accommodate me. I promise." He kisses me all over my face, then whispers, "You were made for me."

I was made for him.

I repeat his words over and over in my head and it relaxes me.

"That's it, *farfalla*, let me see you spread your wings. Let me see you fly." Santino pushes in a little more and I welcome him this time instead of tensing up.

I keep my eyes on his and cup his cheek. "Give me all of you." His eyes flare with heat and he pushes the rest of the way inside me. "Ohmygod," I say in a rush.

My inner muscles clench around him and he groans, pressing his forehead to mine. "You can't do that or this will end way too soon."

"You like that?" I ask, feigning innocence while I do it again.

"Mia," he growls, his eyes sharp.

I smile and lift my head to give him a quick kiss. "You feel so good inside me, Santino." He groans again at my confession and kisses me long and deep while my body adjusts to his size.

Finally, he pulls out a few inches and then slowly pushes back in. I gasp, and he does it again. And again. Then he pulls out to the tip and pushes all the way back inside at the same slow pace.

"Santino," I moan, my entire body on fire. He feels so, so good, but I'm chasing something and he's going too slow to keep up. "More," I choke out. "Faster."

"Not yet, *farfalla*. I promised slow the first time." He kisses his way to my ear. "I promised to make love to you."

I think my heart is going to burst from how careful he's trying to be with me while keeping his promise.

"I know, but–" I say, and he cuts me off with another long, slow stroke of his cock. I arch my back, smashing my chest to his. "Please!" I beg. "It's so good, but I need more. I need you to go faster. I need…I don't know," I say, frustrated. I grab his hair and pull him back to my lips, trying to convey to him how wound-up I am and how much I need him to help me…shatter. Explode. Fly. Be lit on fire. *Everything*.

"You need me to fuck you, my bride?"

"Yes!" I cry out, wrapping my legs around his waist. "Fuck. Me. Now."

"What my bride wants, I give her." Pulling out of me,

Santino pauses for a moment, ensuring my eyes are on his. "And she looks so sexy taking my cock for the first time."

He slams back inside me in a single quick motion and I cry out, causing him to go still inside me. "No, no, no," I chant. "Don't stop. Keep going." I scratch my nails across his shoulders.

"Oh, I plan to," he assures me, rolling his hips so he rubs against my clit.

Santino thrusts into me over and over again, picking up speed each time, until I'm completely lost.

I'm completely gone.

I'm climbing higher and higher, hoping to finally touch heaven before I freefall back down to reality.

Santino is fucking me like a man possessed, or rather obsessed, is the greatest pleasure I've ever felt. I never want it to end, while at the same time, I need to come desperately.

He cups the side of my neck and keeps his dark eyes on mine as he fucks me, taking and giving with every thrust.

"Give in to me, Mia. Let me see my *farfalla* fly."

"Fly with me," I manage to say, and Santino growls.

He reaches between us to rub my clit and I see stars. I manage to touch heaven, and float there for a moment, before Santino thrusts into me again and I burst apart into a million stars of my own – on fire and floating amongst the abyss of space.

He thrusts into me one more time, then stills, groaning into my neck. I have no idea if it feels the same way for him, but as he continues to make slow circles around my clit, he keeps me floating in space as little aftershocks pulsate through my body and I continue to convulse around him.

I don't realize my nails are digging into his back until I loosen my hold on him and go slack beneath him, completely spent.

"How are you?" Santino asks, kissing me all over my face. "Are you okay?"

"More than okay," I tell him, my voice soft. The blood rushing through my head finally starts to settle and I can hear the pounding of our hearts plastered together. "Thank you."

Santino chuckles. "Thank you?"

"For checking to make sure I'm okay." I run my fingers up and down his back. "Thank you."

"I wasn't too rough for your first time?"

I slide my hands over his shoulders and up his neck to cup his face. His dark brown eyes are slightly lighter somehow, and full of a mix of worry and wonder.

"No, you weren't. I wanted you to give me exactly what you did, and it was perfect. I promise. Cross my heart and hope to–" I'm in the middle of making the X mark over my heart when he swoops down and grabs my finger between his teeth, cutting me off mid phrase. I squeal when he bites down.

"Don't even think of finishing that stupid saying," he says roughly. "I hate it and I don't want to think of you…you know."

"Dying?"

"Shh," he hushes, kissing me quiet. "I said don't say it."

Laughing, I caress his cheek. "Okay." I look between his

eyes, debating if I should ask the question on the tip of my tongue.

"Ask me whatever is on your mind."

"How did you–?"

"It's written all over your face."

"I was wondering if it feels the same for you."

"Sex?"

"Yes. Well, kind of. I was thinking more about the orgasm part."

"How does it feel for you?" he asks, and I can see in his eyes that he's *very* interested in my answer.

"The pressure in me builds up until you set me off, and I'm falling and flying like I'm a million burning stars floating in space."

Santino's eyes soften and crinkle at the edges. "That sounds pretty fucking awesome."

I burst out laughing and he smiles that million-dollar smile that can get me to do anything. "For me, it's a fire that travels down my spine. My cock gets even harder and swells right before I come. With you, my bride, I've never come harder in my life, and that means I saw fucking stars when I came, losing myself to you. And the feeling of your pussy squeezing me and pulsating around me as you orgasmed…" He shakes his head in disbelief. "It was like a tight hug for my cock, and I can't say I've ever had a better hug in my life. I told you, you were made for me." Santino kisses me long and slow to show me just how much. He slips out of me and I groan, missing him already.

"I'm going to get a warm washcloth to clean you up, my

bride. Just relax."

My eyes start to droop immediately, but I moan in appreciation when he gently takes care of me and then comes back to hold me as I drift off into a blissful sleep.

CHAPTER 23
Santino

Mia Antonucci.

My wife. My heart. My weakness. My undoing.

We spent two days in bed and I explored every inch of her body, learning everything it's capable of doing and feeling.

Mia let me fuck her until she passed out, and then I'd wake her up with my mouth on her because I needed to taste her and touch her, but knew she was sore and needed a break.

Her screams and moans were the soundtrack on repeat for two days, and her naked body my canvas to create art with my hands and mouth.

"Wake up, my bride," I whisper in her ear, planting kisses

down her neck and across her shoulder.

"No," she mumbles, curling into me and snuggling closer.

"I ran a hot bath for you and I'm about to make you breakfast."

She opens one eye and peers up at me. "Pancakes?"

"If that's what you want."

"It is."

"Then let's get you in the bath. I know you must be sore."

"Just a little." She shimmies her hips against me and I slide out of bed before I decide I need to fuck her again.

"Nope. Come on, my bride." I lift her in my arms and carry her into the bathroom, lowering her right inside the waiting hot water.

She sighs on contact. "That's nice. Are you going to join me?"

"I'm going to make you breakfast," I remind her.

"You can do that after, can't you? This tub is more than big enough for the both of us." Mia runs her hands back and forth over the sides of the tub and bites her lip, giving me her sexy eyes.

"Is it?" Her eyes drop to my already half-hardened cock, which is getting harder the longer she stares. "Mia."

"Hmm?" she hums, feigning innocence by fluttering her eyes at me. She's become quite the little vixen over the past two days.

"You've learned I can't resist you, haven't you?"

"You've mentioned a few times how you'd do anything for me, so I thought that extended to this. If not…" She shrugs. "I can always just clean myself."

"That's an offer I'll never turn down, *farfalla*."

I climb in behind her and she settles against me, leaning her head against my shoulder. I grab the soap from the teak table beside the tub and lather the luffa generously.

Starting at her shoulders, I swipe down each of her arms, across her chest, and down the center of her breasts to her lower abdomen.

"Mmm," she hums, her eyes closed.

I watch her nipples pucker as they peek out of the water with her every intake of breath, and I can't resist giving her pussy a little scrub so she can feel the bite of rough pain with the pleasure.

Mia gasps and then moans. "Santino."

"Shh, baby, let me clean my dirty wife."

"Santino!" She slaps my leg and presses back into me, sloshing water over the lip of the tub and uncomfortably trapping my dick against her back.

I grunt in pain and she covers her mouth with her hand. "Oh, my God, I'm sorry! I forgot about…your…uhm…"

"Cock?" I offer, and she giggles.

"Yes, that."

"Say it, baby," I demand gruffly in her ear, running the luffa over her nipples again. "I like hearing your sweet mouth say dirty things."

"Cock," she whispers, and my dick jerks. "I felt that."

I kiss the side of her neck. "I wanted you to. Your dirty words make my cock want to be inside you and stay there."

"That can be arranged," she offers, and my dick jumps again, wanting that more than anything.

"I wish, my bride, but you're sore, and I'm here to take care of you right now."

"I'm not stopping you from doing that, am I?" she asks innocently, gently leaning back against me again.

Smiling, I continue to wash her flawless skin. My arms are only able to reach down to her knees, so Mia takes the luffa from me and gets the rest of her legs and feet, then hands it back to me. I slide it back up her thighs and she brings her knees up, letting them fall to the sides.

I swirl my tongue around the shell of her ear. "Is that an invitation, *farfalla*?"

"Mmhmm." Mia wraps her arm up around my neck, raising her perfect tits out of the water so I can see how fucking hard her nipples are and how desperate she is for more of my touch.

Goddamn.

I hoped she'd need me like this, and it's a goddamn revelation to have the only wish of my life come true.

I run the luffa over her pussy and Mia shudders, lifting her hips to meet my hand.

"Hold still, my bride, or you'll splash water everywhere. Let me take care of you."

"I can't help it," she practically whines, and I smile.

She has me doing a lot more of that, too. Smiling. Nothing much in my life had me smiling before Mia. She's given me a new purpose in life and I'm never letting her go.

I continue to work her up with the luffa, her hips rocking along with me.

I bite the side of her neck and she moans. "Play with your tits, Mia," I demand, and her hands immediately cup herself. She kneads her mounds and I bite down on her neck. "Now pinch your nipples."

I rub her faster and she does as I tell her, pinching and rolling her hard peaks between her fingers.

"It's…" she pants. "I need you to…" she starts to say, then stops.

"Tell me what you need."

"I need you inside me. I feel empty."

Fuck.

Her confession has my dick leaking and aching to be back inside her.

"I don't have a condom in here," I rasp, pushing the luffa away and replacing it with my fingers, rubbing circles around her hard and swollen clit.

She shakes her head. "I don't care. I need you."

"Mia," I growl. "You don't know what you're saying." I slip two fingers inside her easily, and she clenches around me, trying to hold me inside her. "You know I'm all in with you. I'd have knocked you up two days ago if I thought that's what you wanted, but you need time."

"Stop insisting you know what I need." I work my fingers in and out of her, then add a third finger, and she lets out a long moan. "Santino." She moans my name and it's so fucking sexy, I want to give in and give her what she's asking for. "I've been on birth control since I was eighteen," she admits.

I freeze. "What? Why?"

"Don't stop," she begs, but I keep still. "I had bad acne and horrible periods," she finally tells me when I won't move again. "It helps."

"And you weren't going to tell me that?"

"It's not your business," she says, trying to get herself off by continuing to play with her tits. I band my arm over her chest to keep her from doing just that. "Hey!" she protests.

"You don't think it's a husband's business to know that his wife takes birth control?" She remains quiet, but tries to move her hips, so I remove my fingers and press down on her pussy so she can't move an inch. "Especially when they've been having marathon sex for days and have gone through countless condoms. Are you telling me I could've felt my wife bare, with nothing between us, and you weren't going to tell me?"

"I just did."

"Only because we're in the bath and you're desperate for my cock."

"Fuck you," she growls, angry Mia making a return.

"I plan to, my gorgeous wife." I bite her neck, making her moan. "I just need to ask one more question."

"What?" she growls again, her anger making me even harder. I love how feisty she gets.

"Why didn't you tell me?"

"Seriously?"

"Deadly serious, Mia."

She tries to move her hands over her tits and her hips against my hand, but I've got her pinned in place. She huffs out a frustrated breath. "Because I didn't know if I could be with you like that. I don't know where you've been. It's called being safe."

"I'm clean, Mia. I got tested at my yearly physical a few months ago, and as I've told you, I haven't been with, or looked at, another woman since I first saw you. And just so you know," I add, taking her earlobe between my teeth, feeling her shiver in my arms. "I've never not used a condom."

"I'd be your first?" she asks softly, and my heart twists at the hopeful emotion I hear in her words.

"Yes, Mia, you'll be my first. If you let me."

"Please," she pleads, her eager desperation making me hard as fucking steel and just as desperate.

"Hearing you beg, *farfalla*..." I say low in her ear, pressing her against me even more. "Can you feel what it does to me? You know I want to give you everything you desire. And if you desire me inside you with nothing between us but our need to be as close as possible, then it'll be my pleasure. Literally."

I take my hands away and lift her, lining my cock up at her entrance.

"Grip the edge of the tub, baby."

She does, and I grab her chin, turning her face to the side so I can see the crazed need in her eyes for myself. I kiss her hard and pull her down onto my cock as I thrust up inside her.

Mia groans and bites down on my lip.

"Fuck," I grunt, and grip her hips with both hands,

holding her down on me. "Do you feel me, *farfalla*? Do you feel all of me? Because you feel like fucking heaven."

Her breathing is erratic. "I feel you. You feel like heaven, too. Deeper. Bigger."

"And I'll feel even deeper like this," I tell her, lifting her up and switching her from having her feet flat down beside my legs, to a kneeling pose and then sit her back down on my cock.

"Ahh!" she cries out, arching her spine and dropping her head back. "Yes!"

I grip her hips and guide her up and down my cock, letting her get used to the new position.

"Santino," she moans. "So good."

My ego inflates along with my heart, feeling like a goddamn superhero for giving it to my girl so fucking good.

I know the moment she wants to take over and I loosen my grip just the slightest, letting her ride me.

The way her back and arm muscles flex every time she lifts up and drops down on me has me mesmerized. The top of her ass peeks out of the water every time she does, too, and it's a fucking sight to see.

"You look so beautiful fucking me, Mia," I praise, and her inner walls squeeze around me like a vice. "You're making it very difficult to not take control and fuck you from behind so I can see more of your perfect ass jiggle as I slam into you and hear your screams echo around me."

"Santino," she moans. "Yes," she manages to say, her rhythm faltering after my words. "Fuck me like that. Please."

"You know I love when you talk dirty, my bride. Now get

on your knees and grab the end of the tub." I shove her forward and she clutches the edge opposite of me. Up on my knees behind her, I slap her ass and grab her round cheeks, spreading them apart so I can thrust right back home inside her tight pussy.

Yes.

Home.

Where I belong.

I fuck her hard, the water splashing all around us and onto the floor. Her moans turn into screams, and I go blind with the crazed need to fuck her until I'm imprinted inside her. I want her to feel me for days. I want her to know that not telling me she was on the pill has kept us from fucking like this for two days.

A little punishment with her pleasure.

The telltale fire starts to travel down my spine, starting at the base of my neck, and settling at the base of my spine. I fight it for as long as I can. I want to keep fucking her. I *have to* keep fucking her.

I fuck her through her first orgasm, almost blowing my load with how tight she's squeezing me. Her pussy is pulsating around me, but I keep going.

I know her body now, and I can feel another orgasm building in her, so I drop a little lower to fuck her upwards at a slightly different angle that I know will hit that spot deep inside her that will be her undoing.

Over and over, I hit that spot, and her screams grow louder and louder. Music to my fucking ears.

"Give me another one, Mia," I growl out, and she wails out a scream that has her body vibrating and her pussy sucking my orgasm right out of me.

Groaning, I let her take me with her and slam into her one last time as my cum shoots into her, coating her insides and marking her as mine, and only mine.

I've never done that with any other woman and it feels like the most powerful gift I can give Mia. She's giving me all her firsts and I'm giving her all the ones I have left.

CHAPTER 24
Mia

I can't move or take a step without feeling the aftereffect of Santino taking me the way he did in the bathtub.

He was like an uncaged beast, not holding anything back, and I took it all, wanting it all, and loving it all.

Santino went to make the breakfast he promised me, but I've been slow to get dressed and meet him in the kitchen. It feels like I've fought a battle, physically and mentally, and now that I'm in the calm aftermath, I'm a little lost.

I'm so sore, I put on yoga pants and an oversized sweatshirt, not trying to attract Santino in any way. I can't take anymore today. In the best way possible, that is. But still.

I slowly shuffle out of the room and down the hall. "Mmm," I hum, "the coffee smells good."

I sidle up onto one of the stools around the kitchen island and Santino pours me a cup from the pot and places it in front of me with a small carton of creamer.

"Thank you." I wiggle to adjust myself and wince.

"What's wrong? Are you hurt? Did I hurt you?" The worry in his voice is sweet.

"Just sore. I'll be fine." I pour a little cream into my coffee and stir it. "I don't mind, actually," I add quietly, feeling my cheeks heat.

Santino moves my hair over my shoulder and runs his fingers across my cheeks. "You don't mind, huh?" he asks with a little smug smirk.

"No, I don't. But I can't do *that* again for a while. At least for the rest of today."

"Understood, my bride." Giving me a gentle kiss on the lips, he goes back to cooking me breakfast and I prop my elbows on the counter and watch him. He's only in a pair of low-slung sweatpants, which leaves his perfectly sculpted back, arms, chest, and abs as my view with my morning coffee.

He looks quite domestic, and I quite like it. I like it a lot.

I knew I was falling in love with him on our date a few days ago, but this weekend has connected us in a way that I can't even put into words.

I gave him my body, soul, and heart every time he touched me, slide into me, and made me float amongst the stars. I handed him all the pieces of me he needs to break me beyond repair, and after this morning, I'm a little scared.

I'm scared that I've given into him too quickly and too wholly. I'm scared he's too good to be true and this is all going to blow up in my face.

"What are you thinking?" Santino asks, placing a plate of pancakes in front of me, shaking me from my thoughts.

"Nothing," I say quickly, reaching for the maple syrup. He grabs my wrist before I can, though, and brings my hand to his mouth to kiss each pad of my fingertips.

"Don't lie. Not after everything. Tell me."

"I'm scared."

"Of?"

"You. This. Us. Take your pick. I'm scared that I'm giving my everything to a man who has the power to destroy me." I look away from his penetrating gaze, but he grabs my chin and turns my face back to look at him.

"Intimacy is scary, Mia. Giving yourself to someone isn't easy or something that should be done lightly. But when two people choose to do it together, equally giving themselves to the other and being vulnerable, then it's a little less scary, right?"

"So, we're doing it together?"

"Yes, my bride, we're doing it together," he assures me. "And I'll keep telling you no matter how many times you need to hear it, that I'm serious about us. There's no second shoe that'll drop. There's no ulterior motive. There's no second guessing. There's no backtracking. There's only us, moving forward and figuring it all out together. Do you think you can do that with me?"

"Yes, I can," I tell him, and the corners of his lips lift in a boyish little smile. "And I want to."

Santino leans down and kisses each of the corners of my mouth before kissing me fully, sealing the deal.

I spin towards him and wrap my arms around his neck, pulling him down to kiss him properly. I kiss him like he deserves. I give him everything I can't say yet in this kiss, showing him that I'm so far down this path with him that I didn't even realize I can't see the starting line anymore.

"Eat your pancakes before they get cold, *farfalla*," he murmurs against my lips, kissing each corner again.

CHAPTER 25
Santino

"You look happy, San," Emilio says, joining me on Albie's couch to watch the game.

"I am, man." I take a drag from my beer and settle back into the couch, propping my feet up on the coffee table. I spent yesterday relaxing with my wife, letting her body recover from the absolute primal and mind-blowing fucking we did all weekend, and then I held her all night and woke her up to fuck her slow and lazily before going to my meeting with Leo this morning.

Emilio, Albie, and I have a Monday night football tradition to maintain, and Mia insisted I keep it.

"It's going well with Mia, then?"

I can't stop the smile from taking over my face. "Yeah, it is."

"Good, brother. You deserve to be happy."

"So do you and Albie."

"Eh, we'll find women when we find them. Or maybe we'll take a page from your playbook and just marry a random hot chick and fall in love."

"She was never random," I confess, and he goes quiet, his attention now on me and not the TV.

"What do you mean?" Emilio asks.

"I made sure marrying Mia was a part of my deal with Leo. I could've negotiated without her, but I've wanted her for months. I saw her at Leo's wedding and have been waiting until the right moment to take her. The opportunity came sooner than I thought, actually."

"Are you fucking serious, San?" he asks incredulously.

I look at him and laugh. "Yeah, why? You're looking at me like I'm insane."

"Because you are. Hey, Al, get in here!" he yells over his shoulder.

"What? I'm in the middle of making pizza."

Damn, I don't want to interrupt him when he's cooking. For all that he lacks in time management skills and seriousness, he makes up for in his cooking abilities. When our mom would be off on one of her trips or out to dinner with her friends, leaving us home with dad, Albie was usually in charge of cooking. He taught himself when we were tired of take-out, and while we all can hold our own in the kitchen, he's the best out of the three of us.

"Santino just told me something quite interesting that you need to hear."

"Really?" his eyes light up, ready to have something good to hold over my head.

"Yes, it turns out he orchestrated marrying Mia this entire time. She wasn't just the one the Carfanos offered up on the chopping block as a prize for helping them and joining our families. She was requested by our dear older brother. Insisted upon, actually."

"Was she now? Well, well, well, isn't that interesting?"

"Yes, it is. He saw her at Leo's wedding and waited for the right moment to take her."

"Jesus," I groan, letting my head fall back on the couch. "You better not go around telling people this shit."

"Does Mia know?" Albie asks.

"Yes."

His eyes widen in surprise. "And she still wants you?"

"Fuck off. Yes, she does."

"Huh, I have to rethink how I go about getting women from now on," Albie jokes, contemplating.

"I knew she was the one and mine from the moment I saw her. I had to have her. I married her so she'd be tied to me and couldn't just walk away when I spouted my crazy."

"Fuck, man," Emilio says, looking at me like he doesn't know me. "I've never been that crazy over a woman and I hope I never am."

"Same," Albie agrees. "I don't need crazy. I need easy and often. That's it."

"Shut up and get back in the kitchen. We're hungry," I tell him, and his easy grin disappears.

"You're lucky I know ladies love a man who can cook or I'd take offense to that and punch you in the goddamn face."

Emilio and I laugh and drink our beer. "Don't punch me, brother. I don't want to explain a black eye or busted lip to my wife. She might not look at me like a prime piece of meat anymore if I was marred."

Emilio laughs harder. "Chicks love battle wounds, brother."

"It's true, they do," Albie agrees. "The scar above my eyebrow has always made the ladies think I'm a little dangerous and can hold my own in a barfight."

"You got that scar from when we were kids and Emilio clocked you in the head with a Hot Wheels car when you were being annoying."

"Yeah, well, I don't tell them that," he grumbles, walking back into the kitchen.

"He's so easily thrown," Emilio jokes, shaking his head.

"He'll never outgrow being our annoying little brother. We have to remind him occasionally."

We clink beer bottles and go back to watching the game.

During halftime, Emilio brings up the topic I don't care to discuss. "I can't believe Javi is making you go on the run on Wednesday to prove your loyalty or some bullshit like that."

"Yeah, it's been years since I did that shit, and now I have to do it again to prove myself like I had to do with dad. I'm going to look like a fucking pussy Boss who has to prove himself like a goddamn soldier."

"I can go with you instead of one of our guys as backup. Maybe it'll seem less pussy-like if I do."

"No, definitely not. I'll be fine. I'm going to drive the truck going to Philly. It's a safer route and a more discreet warehouse drop off than Newark or New Haven. I obviously can't drive the truck just going to the Brox. I'd look like even more of a pussy avoiding doing my job if I take the shortest route."

"I guess." He shrugs.

"Leo and I talked to the Melccionas this morning, and they'll have two men riding along in each truck. The delivers should be quick and easy with the extra hands to help unload."

"You think Javier will approve of the deal?"

"He will. He's getting a discount working with the Melccionas while still working with a reputable family."

"You're more confident than I am. I don't know." Em shakes his head in disbelief. "Something about Javi has me thinking he's agreeing too easily or doesn't plan on saying yes in the end and just has you going on the run so he can fuck with you."

"Fuck with me how? What is he going to do? He wouldn't risk anything happening to his product, trust me on that."

"I guess." I can still see the skepticism in his eyes, but he doesn't question me further.

CHAPTER 26
Santino

"What smells so good, *farfalla*?" I ask, walking into the kitchen. I was over at Emilio's going over plans for tonight's run and any contingency plans, just in case.

Mia gives me a warm smile and I'm struck by her beauty all over again like it's the first time. She looks so at ease and comfortable in my apartment, and I can't wait to see her in the home she creates for us. "I just took out the loaf of bread I baked to go with dinner. How does honey garlic chicken sound?"

"Delicious, baby, but I won't be home for dinner tonight." Her smile falters and I wrap my arms around her, kissing her until she sags against me. "I'm sorry. I have something important to take care of tonight or I wouldn't dare turn down a meal made by my beautiful wife. I'll be home late, so don't wait up for me. I'll wake you up with my mouth on your sweet pussy, though, if you don't mind." I kiss her again, and she hops up into my arms, wrapping her legs around me as I set her on the counter.

"I don't mind. I insist, actually."

"Good." I nuzzle her neck, inhaling her floral scent that makes me think of her running through a field of wildflowers with a wide smile as she calls over her shoulder for me to catch her.

"I ordered a few things for the house today," she tells me, scratching her nails through my hair. Damn, that feels good.

"You did? What did you get?"

"I decided to start with the living room since I didn't get a chance to have a tour of the upstairs yet." Her cheeky grin has my dick remembering exactly why I didn't get a chance to show her the entire house.

"I can take you back there anytime to finish the tour." I wink. "I'll also give you a key and the security code so you can go whenever you'd like, too."

"Thank you. I had fun searching for the perfect things today."

"I'm glad, baby. I hope you bought some expensive things, too."

She smirks, running her finger down my jawline. "I did."

"Good. Now, I have to change for my meeting. You want

to come watch me?" Mia bursts out laughing and pats my cheek.

"Yes, husband, I'd very much like to watch you undress and then re-dress. It's a free show I wouldn't pass on."

I lift her off the counter and carry her to our bedroom, loving the feel of her wrapped around me like a coiled snake.

I place her down the bed and she sits cross-legged with her eyes roving over my body with a cute little grin while I undress. I leave my briefs on and she frowns, making me laugh.

"Don't worry, *farfalla*. I'm all yours later."

"You don't have time for me?" She pouts, looking at me with sad puppy eyes and a frown.

"Oh, no. Don't give me that look. I have to meet *your* family in an hour. I don't have time to fuck you, shower, and get over there in time."

"What if I told you I've been thinking about you all day and could easily come in a minute if you fucked me hard enough."

Groaning, I hit my forehead against the doorframe of the closet. "Mia," I say painfully, my cock already begging to be inside her. "You're killing me."

"I'm sure you need to focus during your meeting tonight, right? That might be difficult if you're not taken care of first. My family might notice and want to kill you."

I look at her from beneath my lashes and she grins victoriously, scrambling off the bed and shedding her clothes in two seconds flat before running to me and jumping back into my arms.

"I've turned you into a monster," I say right before I slam my mouth down on hers and press her against the wall. She reaches between us and takes my cock out, lining me up at her entrance, but I pause to tell her, "I'm going to fuck you hard and fast, and you're going to come when I tell you to come. If you're not there when I am, then your punishment for this untimely seduction will be to wait until I get home later to come all over my cock. Understand?"

"Yes, fine. Got it. Please fuck me now."

She's so polite while being so dirty. I fucking love this woman.

With that declaration on the forefront of my mind, I thrust into her with a savage force, and Mia cries out in a mix of pain and pleasure.

"That's right, baby. Take me like the good wife you are."

Her eyes are wild and her nails dig into my shoulders as I fuck her like an animal. She needs the quick release, and as it turns out, I do as well.

I love that if I leave her for the day, she gets herself all riled-up by just thinking about me.

She's fucking perfect and I fucking love her.

I take her hard and fast, and with her tight, hot pussy hugging me like I haven't been inside her in days or weeks rather than just this morning, it takes me less than a minute before I'm ready to fill her with my cum.

I tilt her hips back and drop down a little to be able to hit her deeper and reach that spot I know will get her to come in seconds. And I'm right. I feel her inner walls start to flutter around me while she gives me a deep moan I feel vibrate through me.

"Come with me," I demand. "Now."

I slam into her one final time and bury myself as deep as I can go, no doubt hitting her fucking cervix as I fill her greedy pussy full of my seed.

Mia cries out as she milks my cock for all it has as her nails claw across the width of my shoulder blades. Fuck me, I hope she leaves marks. I'll wear them with the same amount of pride as a horny teenager who just got his first hickey. Even if no one sees them, I'll still be carrying around the evidence of our fucking while I'm out doing the last fucking thing I want to be doing tonight.

"I guess that'll hold me over until you get home later," she says casually, but her glazed-over eyes are giving away the fact that I fucked her into oblivion.

I carry her over to our bed and lay her down and tuck her in. Her eyes flutter closed and I kiss her cheek. "Yes, *farfalla*," I whisper in her ear. "It'll hold me over until I get home later, too."

Grinning at her already sleeping form, I quickly clean myself up in the bathroom and get dressed. I can't dress how I usually do, in a suit and tie, to deliver crates of coffee, so I go for black jeans, a black hoodie, and my black motorcycle boots I haven't worn in forever. Probably because I haven't taken my bike out of the garage in years.

I switch my license in my wallet out with another from my safe in the closet that has a fake name. If something goes wrong and we get pulled over, I don't need my last name giving the cops a dead giveaway that something illegal is going on and give cause for a search.

Slipping my wallet into my back pocket, I close the safe and cover it with my stack of shoe boxes again.

I give Mia another kiss on the cheek and whisper, "Rest, my beautiful wife. I'll see you later."

When she said she wasn't going to fight herself on how she felt anymore, she seriously meant it. My girl can't get enough of my cock, and I can't wait for the day she takes me in her mouth and I fuck her in her ass. Then I'll really have staked my claim on every inch of her body and I'll know I've filled her with my cum in every way I can.

Damn it, I can't think about that right now. I need to focus on tonight.

Lou and the men he's sending on the run with me tonight are meeting me and my men at the Carfano building before we head over to the warehouse by the port terminal so we can go over the route, plan, and procedure one more time.

"Santino, good to see you again," Lou says, shaking my hand. "These are the men joining you tonight. Four trucks and two men each."

"They're not big trucks. The cab can only fit three men comfortably, so one will need to ride in the back with the product. That okay?"

"Yeah, that'll be fine. They'll do whatever you tell them to so we can get this deal done."

"Perfect." I look at his men and give them a nod of

approval. "Let's go over each of your routes again now that we're all together."

I pair the men up and reiterate to them to take a different route than last time to avoid tolls and major roads with cameras, and what to do once they get there.

Leo, Luca, and Nico sit and listen while I take the lead. They're staying back and waiting for my call later to let them know it went well and we can set up a meeting with Javi to have him meet Lou to finalize the deal.

"If everyone's good, then let's head out." We pair up in SUVs so that we don't draw too much attention with too many cars.

I turn the radio on so that no one gets the idea of talking to me on the drive. I don't care to chitchat or shoot the shit. I'm pissed I'm here and would rather be having dinner with Mia.

We pull right into the warehouse by the port that holds the trucks. Every month, my men go to the port and pick up the crates from the shipping containers and bring them here to house them until the night we do our run.

I climb out of the car and Javi emerges from the shadows with two of his men. "Santino, I'm so glad you're keeping your word."

"I always keep my word, Javi. You know that."

"*Sí*, of course. Introduce me to my potential new drivers."

"This is Ronnie and Caleb. They'll be riding with me." The others arrive and join us so I can introduce them all to Javi.

"Truck one, three, and four can leave now," I instruct. "I'll head out last."

We all do our cursory checks of the trucks to make sure there's nothing wrong on the outside that will get us pulled over.

"Alright, let's head out boys."

We're going to the warehouse on the outskirts of Philly that will then primarily distribute to Philly, Camden, and Trenton. The Newark warehouse in Jersey will distribute to Newark, Elizabeth, and Patterson. The Bronx warehouse is for a lot of the city, and the New Haven warehouse is for most of the North East.

At the warehouses, the drugs are handed over to men who work for Javier, who then cut and package it to be sold to various gangs, organizations, and high-volume dealers who then sell it to their customers, and so on and so forth. We're an important link in the chain, but it's past time to sever that link.

To avoid the tolls and cameras on I-95 and the Turnpike, we take a longer route that's going to take us over two hours.

"We're five minutes out, Boss," Darren, one of my men, informs me.

"Finally." My ass hurts and I need to stretch my legs, but I'm not admitting that, or I'll sound like the old man of the group.

I turn onto a block that's lined in warehouses, both abandoned and occupied, and when I get to the one we want, whoever is monitoring the cameras spots us, and the garage style door lifts to let us drive in.

The door shutters down behind us and I get a bad feeling in the pit of my stomach in a matter of seconds. It's dark and quiet. Too dark and too quiet.

"I don't like this," I say quietly.

"It's never like this. We're always greeted when we come in," Darren says back, just as quietly.

"You packing?"

"Of course."

"How about you, Caleb?"

"I am," he says calmly.

"Message Ronnie in the back to stay still and quiet. Just in case something happens, he needs to stay with the product," I tell him, and he discreetly pulls his phone out to text him. "Get ready for anything, boys." I pull my gun from behind my back and flip the safety off.

I'd back the fuck out of here if the reinforced barricade of a door wasn't just closed to keep us in. There's no way this truck will break it down.

I take a breath and scan the darkness in front of us, the headlights not showing anything but a brick wall in front of us.

"Let's fucking do this," Darren says to Caleb. "Boss, you stay in here while I check it out first."

Darren opens his door only as far as he needs to slip out, and Caleb follows right behind him. I'm not a pussy who sits back while others protect me, so I slip out of my door, and that's when all hell breaks loose.

The first bullet rings out, and a searing fire rips through

my shoulder.

FUCK!

I drop low, not knowing where it came from, and roll under the truck. I need to find the fucking light switch in this place to take away their element of surprise.

The pain is easy to ignore, and the moment the lights turn on, I know Darren or Caleb had the same idea as me. I roll out the other side of the truck and put a bullet in the chest of someone aiming their gun at Darren.

More bullets fire off, and I take cover behind a stack of crates that used to hold bags of coffee and cocaine, and pick off men that start to come out of nowhere.

Who the fuck are they?

I need to get the door open and get the fuck out of here.

I start to make my way around the perimeter of the warehouse, ignoring the burning in my shoulder.

It's quiet for a moment and then a series of bullets ring out and I hurry over to the chains that control the door and grab the remote hanging from it. I'm about to press the black button when a bullet rips through my side and I grunt.

FUCK!

This one hit something important.

Goddamn it.

I start to slide down the wall and my vision blurs, but I manage to fire my gun off and hit the two more guys coming at me before my arm feels too heavy to hold my gun up.

"Get the door open and get in the truck!" I hear voices yelling.

"Are they all dead?"

"Yes, get the door and let's go!" the guy yells again, and I close my eyes, needing them to think I'm dead. I feel like I am. Or almost there.

Someone comes next to me and kicks me, then presses the button to open the door. He turns to jog back to the truck and I raise my shaky arm with what strength I have left and fire off two bullets, one of them hitting him in the back and taking him down.

"I thought they were dead!" The truck's engine roars to life and the tires screech as the gas pedal is floored and the truck speeds out in reverse.

I try to move, to do anything, even reach for my phone, but my body won't listen to my brain and I'm motionless on the concrete floor.

The room blurs, and as my eyes close, I send a silent apology to Mia.

Sorry, my bride. I won't make it home. I love you, farfalla.

"Santino! Santino!" a voice yells in the distance. "Fuck! He's over here! Hey, brother, stay with me!"

"Mia," I mouth, trying to say her name.

"Mia's fine, San. Just stay with me. Al, help me get him in the car!"

Emilio? Albie? They're here?

I open my mouth to ask them why, but the ground suddenly rushes out from under me and I groan.

"You're going to be fine, San. We've got you. Don't fucking die. Think of Mia. You just got her."

"Mia," I whisper, and it's her beautiful face I see as I slip into unconsciousness.

I wish I could see her one more time.

CHAPTER 27
Mia

I put the leftovers from dinner in the fridge for Santino when he gets home later and plop down on the couch. I pick up my laptop and start to scroll through websites for things for the house when my phone rings. I smile down at the name.

"Hey, Gia. I haven't talked to you in what feels like forever."

"I know! Aria is here too. You're on speaker."

"Hey, Mia!" Aria shouts. "How's that hot husband of yours?"

"Aria!"

"What? He's hot, you can't deny that. Have you gotten to

experience said hotness yet?"

I smile and feel my cheeks heat even though there's no one here to see my embarrassment "As a matter of fact, yes, I have."

"WHAT?!" they both screech together, and I pull the phone away from my ear. "Tell us everything. Now. Is he there?"

"No, he's out at a meeting or something. I don't know. I know not to ask too many questions."

"Then spill, Mia. We want to know *everything*."

I think I've needed some good girl talk, because everything just spills out of me. Not *everything*, but a lot of what's happened between me and Santino.

We talk for over an hour and they fill me in on their newest campaign ad they booked and club promotions they've attended. I was so envious of their lives for the longest time, but now that I'm with Santino, I honestly can't say I want to be them instead.

Yawning, I lean my head back on the couch and close my eyes. "Alright, guys, I'm tired. I'm going to go to bed now."

"Us too. Call us soon," Gia says.

"And we want to see your new house!" Aria adds.

"I'll give you a tour as soon as Santino finishes giving me mine."

"Ohhhh, yes *'a tour'*. I wish I had a man to give me a tour."

"And with that, goodnight." I roll my eyes and hang up, scooting down on the couch.

I hope Santino makes good on his promise to wake me

up with his mouth when he gets home.

My phone starts buzzing on the table and I pat around with my eyes closed until I find it. I don't even bother opening them to see who it is before answering.

"Hello?" I rasp, my voice thick with sleep.

"Mia," someone says right away, their voice desperate and fraught with worry.

My eyes pop open in a flash and I sit up. "Who is this? What's wrong?"

"It's Emilio. Santino…he…"

Panic seizes me. "What happened to him?"

"He was shot." My vision blurs. "Al and I rushed him to the hospital and he's in surgery now, but they don't know if he'll make it yet. There was so much blood," he adds quietly at the end, lost in the memory.

"Which hospital? I'm on my way."

"Penn Presbyterian."

"Where is that?" I ask frantically. "I don't know that one."

"Philly."

"Why is he in Philly? He said he just had a meeting tonight." I run to our room and change out of my pajamas and into the first thing I find, not caring if it matches or what I look like. "Forget it," I say when he doesn't answer me right away. "I'll be there as fast as I can."

"You don't have to rush. I was just calling to tell you. I don't know how long he'll be in surgery or…"

"Don't fucking say it," I growl. "I'll be there as fast as I can."

I hang up and toss my phone in my purse, then dig in the bowl of keys by the door until I find the ones to the sports car he drove on our first date. I need something fast.

The only thing holding me together is pure adrenaline, and as I wait for the elevator, my legs start to shake, but I hold it together. I have to for Santino.

I'm Mia Antonucci.

I'm the wife of a mob boss, and I'll be damned if I don't fucking act like it when I need to be strong for my husband.

Squaring my shoulders, I step into the elevator and ride it down to the garage. I click the key fob to find the car and then run over to it. I start it up and the engine roars to life. It takes me a few seconds to figure everything out, but when I do, I put the hospital into the GPS and tear out of there.

Please don't die. Please don't die.

I repeat it over and over in my head, needing God to hear me. I can't lose him. Not yet. Not when we just started our lives together.

Pressing down on the gas pedal as soon as I hit the highway, I weave in and out of the lanes to bypass everyone in my way. I get a few honks, but I don't give a shit. And the cops wouldn't dare pull me over right now, either.

My grip on the steering wheel is so tight, that when a call comes through on Bluetooth and I loosen my grip to answer it, my knuckles pop.

"What do you know?" I ask Nico right away when I answer.

"He was ambushed."

Arranged

"Ambushed?!" I yell. "Ambushed doing what? He was supposed to just be in a meeting. What did you guys make him do?"

"We didn't do anything, Mia. This wasn't us."

"Then who?"

"We don't know yet, but Leo, Dante, and I are headed down now in the helicopter and will sort it out. I wanted to call to see if you knew what happened yet and if you're okay."

"No, I'm not okay. My husband has been shot and is in surgery fighting for his life, and he could very well die. I'm far from okay."

Nico falls silent, and all I hear is the whooshing of the helicopter blades in the background. He must think I've gone crazy.

"I have to go. I'm on my way to the hospital now, and I need all my concentration."

"Please drive safe, Mia. We're touching down in five."

"Okay, bye." I hang up, now pissed off.

They had to have known what happened right away if they're almost in Philly already. I must've been an afterthought call by his brothers once they got Santino to the hospital and relayed the situation to everyone more important than me.

I know Santino needs me, though. No one else may know, but I do.

I drive a little faster than before, and shave at least ten or fifteen minutes off the GPS's original estimated travel time.

The moment I pull into the garage beside the ER, I park in the first spot I see and run into the waiting room and straight to the desk with a nurse.

"Please, I need to know where my husband is. Santino Antonucci. He was brought in with a gunshot wound and his brother told me he was in surgery."

She types something on her keyboard. "Yes, he's in surgery right now, but that's all the information I can give you. You can wait in the lounge down the hall for the doctor to come out and tell you more."

"So, he's alive?" I ask tentatively, playing with the keys in my hand.

She gives me a soft smile. "Yes, he is as of right now, and he has one of the best surgeons in the country working on him."

"Okay." I nod. "Thank you."

I blindly walk down the hall to the lounge she referred to and find it empty. His brothers aren't here? They must be meeting Nico to handle whatever went wrong.

Hanging my head in my hands, my adrenaline starts to wear off and I'm shaking. That's when the first tear falls, that then turns into a hundred silent ones.

"Mia." A hand rests on my shoulder and I look up into Vinny's concerned eyes.

I swipe my cheeks with the sleeves of my sweatshirt. "What are you doing here?"

"I wasn't going to let you wait here alone. The others are handling the situation, so I came to sit with you."

"Thank you," I whisper, and he takes the seat beside me, wrapping his arm around me. More tears start to fall when I realize how alone I'll be again if Santino dies.

"It's okay, Mia. It'll all be okay."

"I don't know anything yet. All they'll tell me is he's in surgery."

"I can go find out more if you want me to. I just don't want to leave you alone like this."

"No, go. Please find out anything you can." I practically push him to his feet, and he leaves on a mission.

I watch the clock on the wall as the seconds dial moves smoothly in a circle and the minute hand ticks by ever so slowly. It moves ten times before Vinny comes back.

"What did you find out?"

"He was shot twice. Once in the shoulder, but that was a through and through that was easily stitched up. The other one nicked his liver and caused massive hemorrhaging, which is why he's in surgery."

I cover my mouth with my hands, holding in a sob.

"No, Mia, shhh." Vinny sits back next to me and rubs my back. "They got the bleeding under control and are working on closing him back up."

"So, he'll live?" I ask, needing any sliver of hope to hold onto.

"Yes, he will."

"Oh, thank God." I throw my arms around my brother and hug him like I haven't in years. "Thank you for using you're annoying charms on the nurses for me."

"You're welcome, little sis," he chuckles.

"Have you heard from Nico? He called me while I was

driving and said he was about to touch down with Leo and Dante. How did this happen, Vin? Why was Santino down here?"

Vinny looks away and runs his hand through his hair and rubs the back of his neck. "Just focus on Santino. We'll handle the rest. We'll take care of it, Mia."

I knew he wouldn't tell me.

"I know you will."

CHAPTER 28
Mia

"Mrs. Antonucci?"

My head whips around to see a doctor walk into the lounge, and I jump up out of my seat. "Yes? Any news on my husband?"

"He's out of surgery and stable for now. He'll need to be closely monitored for the next 24 hours to make sure he remains stable."

"But he's alive?"

"Yes, he's alive."

"Thank God," I whisper. "Can I see him?"

"He's being transferred to the ICU now, and then a nurse

will let you know when you can see him."

"Thank you," I gush. "Thank you so much."

"Of course, ma'am." His eyes dart to my brother before leaving.

"Oh, thank God." I collapse back into the seat and scrub my hands over my face.

"You're really worried about him," Vinny says, crossing his arms over his chest.

"Why wouldn't I be?"

"Because we asked you to marry him to help us and you were outraged. What changed?"

I roll my eyes. "A lot has changed, Vin. He's a good man," I defend.

"Are you telling me you're in love with him?" he asks, narrowing his eyes. "I'll fucking kill him if he's made you do anything you—" I hold my hand up to stop him from going there.

"Stop, Vin. Santino hasn't made me do anything I haven't wanted to do."

"Except marry him," he counters.

"Well…" I tilt my head back and forth, unsure how to tell him. "Not exactly."

"The fuck?" he growls.

"Look, Vinny, I appreciate your concern, but I'm exhausted, scared, starving, and feel like my face is coated in tears. I don't want to get into this now, or ever, really. Santino and I are married, and anything aside from that is now no one's business but ours."

He stares down at me, his jaw flexing under the pressure of his clenched teeth, but he doesn't say anything else on the topic.

"I'm going to call Leo to let him know Santino's alive."

"Mrs. Antonucci?" A nurse comes into the lounge a few minutes later.

"Yes?"

"You may see your husband now. He's still unconscious, but you may sit with him."

"Thank you." I stand and follow her around the hospital to his room. The moment I see him lying there, pale and practically lifeless, my hand flies to my mouth to muffle my whimper. "Are you sure he's okay?"

"He made it through the surgery well, and his vitals are great so far."

"It's okay if I sit with him?"

"Yes, and if you need anything, there's a button on his bed and the nurse's station is just down the hall."

"Thank you."

I move one of the chairs that's by the table in the corner to beside the bed, and my legs give out. My eyes rake over every visible part of his body outside of the thin blanket, and I hesitate to touch him, my hand freezing mid-air.

His shoulder is covered in a large white gauze bandage, and my hand shakes as I pull back the edge of the blanket to see his torso completely wrapped in another thick bandage.

I blink away more tears and take a deep, steadying breath.

He's alive. We have more time.

I drop the blanket back down and take his hand, kissing his knuckles and resting my forehead on the back of it, needing to be connected to him.

I fall asleep on him, and it isn't until the nurses come in to check on him that I'm startled awake.

"Sorry, honey, I have to check him," she says apologetically.

"It's okay. I appreciate it."

Standing, I stretch, and then take the time to use the bathroom. I catch a glimpse of myself in the mirror and cringe. There's not much I can do other than splash cool water on my face and toss my unruly hair up into a messy bun.

When I return, the nurse is gone and I take my place in the uncomfortable chair again.

I know he wouldn't leave my side if it were me lying here, so I refuse to leave his.

I look at my wedding rings as I cover his hand with mine. I can't believe how easily I got used to seeing them there, knowing what they represent, and now I don't want to have to take them off.

CHAPTER 29
Santino

That annoying beeping won't shut the fuck up.

I slowly peel my eyes open, blinking until my vision clears.

I'm in the hospital?

Then it all comes rushing back to me.

The run. The ambush. Getting shot. My brothers being there. Wishing I could see Mia one more time.

Mia.

The monitor starts beeping faster. Is she okay? I look around the room, but she's not here.

The door opens and in walks Albie and Emilio.

"Hey, brother. You look like shit," Albie says, stating the

obvious.

"Thanks. I feel like shit, too."

"I'm glad you didn't die," he adds, and Emilio punches him in the arm.

"Shut the fuck up for once, Al."

"It's okay." I laugh, then cough. "Ahh, fuck, that hurts. How long was I out for?"

"It's been almost two days."

"Mia?"

"She hasn't left your side since you came out of surgery. We only just convinced her to go to the hotel room we got her to shower and change. Vinny's fiancé, Lexi, brought her clothes and is keeping her company. Mia insisted she'd be right back, though."

"She was here?"

"Yeah," Al says, his brows furrowed. "Did you think she wouldn't be?"

"I didn't know what to think."

"She's a good one, brother. She was shattered to see you like this."

I clear the lump in my throat and look away. I don't like hearing that my girl has been hurting. I need to see her. I need to talk to her.

"So, tell me what happened. I remember you being there. Why were you there?"

"I didn't like that Javi was making you go on the run, and you didn't want me going with you, so we followed you."

"You followed me the entire way to Philly to make sure

nothing went wrong?"

"Yes."

"Then something went wrong."

"Yeah." Emilio takes the chair that's already next to the bed while Albie drags the other one over to sit beside him. "We couldn't get to you until the door was opened. I'm sorry, San." He rubs his hand over his cheek.

"I'm glad you were there," I tell him. "Thank you for saving me." I look between my younger brothers and take in their tired appearances. "Have you guys slept at all?"

"No. We've been out cleaning everything up and tracking down the truck."

"Tell me everything."

"After we got you in the car, I saw how much blood you were losing and knew you needed a hospital ASAP, and didn't have time to find an alternative kind of medical treatment. We got you here and then called Leo to let him know what happened. He got in his helicopter with Nico and Dante and flew down here. Vinny and Alec drove over from Atlantic City, and once they were all here, we went into action. Leo had his cousin track the phone of the Melcciona guy you had in the back of the truck and found it in a warehouse nearby that they moved the truck to."

"Wait, what about Darren and Caleb?"

Emilio shakes his head. "Sorry, San, they were found dead. So was the guy in the back of the truck. We killed everyone in the warehouse where we tracked the phone, took the truck back, and then Dante blew that shit up."

"He loves blowing shit up," Albie says with a laugh. "He blew up the other warehouse too, to get rid of that mess as well."

"The truck was driven back up to the Newark warehouse to be kept safe, and all the other lifeless *packages* were brought to the Port of Newark. Leo's men handled it." Ah, good. I know the Carfanos have disposal sites all over, but the Port of Newark was probably easiest.

I nod my approval and try to adjust my sitting position, but wince and freeze. "Fuck," I say through clenched teeth.

"You okay? Do you need me to get a nurse?"

"No, I'm fine," I grit out. "I just need to not move. Keep going. Did you find out who ambushed me?"

"We did," Al says.

"Javi was contacted by the Aleksanyan guy trying to bring Leo down. He has eyes everywhere and knew you and Leo went to meet him. The only thing Javi told the guy was that you married into the Carfano family and were now merging businesses, so of course the Albanian took that as a threat to his plans he had for Leo. Javi didn't know that the information he conveyed was going to be used to try and kill you and steal his shipment. He's pissed."

"*He's* pissed?" I seethe.

"He didn't realize who he was talking to. Leo has it taken care of. You're family to him now apparently, and he doesn't take well to attacks on his family."

"No, I don't," Leo says, walking into the room. "It's good to see you're alive and awake, Santino."

"Thanks. What are we doing about Javi and…I don't even know his name?"

"It's Burim. Javi gave me the phone number he used to call him and Stefano found out it was a burner and untraceable, but he used the serial number to find the batch it was bought with and where. The dumbass used his dead cousin's credit card. He's been living here under Hovan's identity since he arrived from Albania. It was easy to track him from there."

"You found him?"

"Yes, we found him. He was hiding out in some little cabin in the woods in North Jersey. I sent five men to take care of him and the two men he had with him, and they cleared the house of everything they had on us and what he was able to gather on you this week."

"You work fast."

"I do."

I clear my throat and wince when I move the wrong way. I hold my hand out to Leo. "Thank you. I'm sorry I couldn't help in the takedown."

"I'm sorry you were almost killed because of a vendetta against me. And I'm sorry about your man, too." I nod my head solemnly. "Javi has agreed to dissolve your contract without any ill will and the Melccionas have still agreed to move forward despite losing two men tonight."

"Thank fuck." In a rare moment of his stone features cracking, Leo smiles at my response.

"Business will be better than ever now, Santino. So long as you take care of Mia."

"Of course. Her happiness is my priority."

"Good to hear," he says approvingly. "Take it easy with recovery. You don't have to worry about the cops, either. I've already got it all taken care of so there won't be an investigation or anyone coming to ask you questions."

The door flies open and in comes my beautiful wife. "Santino?" she calls out, pushing past Leo. Her frantic eyes meet mine, and when she sees I'm awake and looking back at her, her face breaks out in a huge grin and she hurries over to me, throwing her arms over me.

"Ooof," I huff, and she gasps.

"Oh, my God. I'm so sorry! I'm just so happy to see you awake." She cups my cheeks as tears gather in her eyes.

"Don't cry, *farfalla*. I'm okay."

"And I'm okay now that you're awake." She leans down and gives me a sweet, gentle kiss. "I'm sorry I wasn't here."

"It's okay. I was told it was the first time you left the room. You didn't have to stay here the whole time."

"Oh, shut up. Of course I did."

"We'll, uhh, give you two some space," Emilio says, and Mia gives him and Albie a hug.

"Thank you for getting him here in time. I'm so grateful. I owe you big time."

"You don't owe us anything."

"But I wouldn't turn down whatever you think is fair," Albie cuts in, making her laugh.

"Get the fuck out of here so I can be alone with my wife," I growl at my brothers.

"Fine, fine. We'll be back tomorrow."

"I'll leave you two as well. Mia," Leo says, giving her a little bow as a goodbye.

"Thank you, Leo. I don't know what happened after all of this"—she waves a hand at my bandages—"but I know you did everything to make it right." Mia throws her arms around her cousin and he doesn't even hesitate to wrap his around her.

"You know you're like another little sister to me, Mia. I'm sorry about everything that's happened this past month, but it's clear to me that things are going well."

"Very well," she says shyly, her cheeks turning pink as she tucks her hair behind her ears.

Fuck, she's cute.

"I'm glad. And Santino, when the doctor gives you the okay for transport, I can have you moved to our hotel, The Aces, in Atlantic City. We have a great doctor and full medical set-up on one of the floors there for you to recover in. Or, we also have the same set-up in my building in Manhattan. I figure you're a little like me and don't want to spend your days in a hospital when we have a much more comfortable option for you."

"Atlantic City sounds like a fun time. I could sneak out and do a little gambling."

"No, you won't. You'll do exactly what the doctor tells you to do."

"Yes, my wife," I agree, and her eyes soften, along with her whole body as she collapses into the chair beside me.

Leo slips out quietly and Mia takes my hand. "I missed

you," she tells me, and the confession is all I need to tell her mine.

"I love you, *farfalla*."

Mia's eyes immediately fill with tears. "Santino," she whispers. Clutching my hand, she brings it up to cup her cheek and holds it there. "I'm so crazy for falling in love with you, but you're crazy too, so I guess it makes sense."

"I told you, baby, you were made for me. It's fate."

"I think so." Mia leans forward and gives me the sweetest kiss. "Can I tell you a secret?"

"Of course."

"When I was walking down the aisle, and I saw you standing there, so handsome and looking at me like you were already in love with me…" She smiles and kisses my lips again. "I had this overwhelming feeling wash over me."

"And what feeling was that?" I ask her, rubbing my thumb back and forth across her cheek.

Mia gives me a smile that has the monitor I'm hooked up to beeping faster. "That I wanted to marry you. I had no regrets when I said 'I do', and I've had no regrets since."

"Come here," I urge, and she kisses me again. It's not enough, though, so I deepen the kiss and pull her closer.

"I don't want to hurt you," she says, trying to pull away.

"I'll be fine. I just need you."

"You have me."

"Then kiss me like I almost died, *farfalla*. I need to know I'm alive."

And kiss me she does.

Arranged

My wife kisses me like she did that first time – desperate, needy, sloppy, and unhinged. It's fucking perfect, just like her.

CHAPTER 30
Mia
2 months later...

Santino pulls up to our house and I smile at the Christmas lights framing the doorway and swirled down the railings. I wanted our first holiday together to be special, especially after everything that happened, so I worked hard to get the house ready by Christmas Eve.

Santino has worked hard to recover and has *actually* followed the doctor's orders after he was released from the hospital. Of course, I may have threatened to withhold all kissing, touching, and sex if he didn't do as he was told, and that seemed to keep him motivated.

"Do you want to give me a tour?" he asks, placing his hand on my thigh.

"Yes, I'd love to. I put up the decorations with Aria and Gia yesterday and it's perfect."

"I know it is."

Santino opens the car door for me and then we walk up the steps of our home. *Our home.*

I never would have imagined life could be so good a few months ago, but here we are.

We step through the door and I smile. "It feels like home," I say, squeezing Santino's hand.

"It does," he agrees. "It's perfect, *farfalla*. You made us a home."

"Do you think Kat would've done this good of a job if you married her?" I ask playfully, nudging his shoulder.

"Mia," he says sternly.

Laughing, I pat his chest. "Just kidding, my handsome husband. You know you would've seen and met me eventually if you were truly going to marry her. Then all bets would've been off." I smile and lean up to kiss his cheek. "You would've still wanted me and gone after me instead."

"You're fucking right I would've," he growls. "You're my woman, Mia. You were made for me. No one else."

"And you were made for me."

Santino kisses me hard, a back bending kiss that has my legs turning to Jello and my heart in overdrive.

"We haven't christened the house yet," I say, breathless. "I'll let you pick where."

"Mia," he rasps, nuzzling my neck. "I've thought a lot about where and how I'd have you in here."

A shiver runs down my spine. "And which won out?"

"I want to finish what we started in the kitchen that first time."

"That's all I've thought about every time I've been here." I step away from him. "Maybe I shouldn't let it be so easy for you. I could pretend I'm the good little virgin again."

"Baby." He gives me a look that has my panties flooding. "You still are my good little virgin. I've dirtied you a little. But not nearly enough."

"If you catch me, you can have your wicked way with me," I taunt, and take off down the hall towards the kitchen. I knew I wouldn't get far, and in a matter of seconds, Santino's arm is banded around my stomach and he's lifting me in the air and dropping me down on the kitchen island.

"Caught you," he rasps in my ear and I lock my arms and legs around him.

"Because I let you."

"Can I unwrap you now, *farfalla*? I want my Christmas present early."

"Depends. Do you think you're on the naughty or nice list this year?"

"Definitely naughty." Santino licks the shell of my ear and bites down. "You're about to find out just how much, my wife."

"That's what I was hoping you'd say," I tell him, and he scrapes his teeth down my neck. Moaning, I scratch my nails through his hair and he sucks on the curve where my neck meets my shoulder. "Santino, wait."

"No, *farfalla*. No waiting. I need you."

I pull on his hair and bring his head back so he'll look at me. "How badly?"

"What?" he asks, his eyes dark and searching mine.

"How badly do you need me?"

He gives me a scorching look. "Very badly, baby."

"Then beg me." I smirk, scratching my nails down his cheek. "I want to hear my husband beg like he did on our wedding night. In fact…" I shrug my coat off my shoulders and lift my sweater over my head, revealing the red version of the white lingerie I wore on our wedding day. "Does this look familiar?"

Santino looks at me like he wants to tear the delicate fabric from my body like a caveman.

"Yes," he croaks. "You look like my wedding present, but for Christmas." He runs a finger along my ribcage under the lace trim.

"Ah, ah, ah," I protest, shaking my head. "No touching yet. Not until I hear the magic words, dear husband."

Santino's jaw flexes and he fists his hands to keep from touching me.

"Mia," he purrs seductively. "*Farfalla*. My beautiful wife. I need to touch you. I need to taste you. I need to see all of you. Please, baby. Let me unwrap you and devour you. Let me fuck you right onto the naughty list. I'm begging you, *farfalla*."

I smile triumphantly. "Just as sweet as the first time. I

believe you've earned your gift now, Mr. Antonucci."

Santino palms my breasts and my head falls back with a relieved sigh.

"I was never one to carefully unwrap my presents, though," he says, then grips the cups of my bra and tears it down the middle. "That's better," he praises, kissing me hard.

I push his coat and suit jacket off and grab ahold of the opening of his shirt and yank it apart. Well, I try to, but it doesn't budge. "Damnit," I grunt, making Santino chuckle as he kisses his way down my neck. "I always ripped into my presents too, but…" I tug again and manage to pop only one button.

"Let me, Mrs. Antonucci." He gently pushes my hands away. "I wouldn't want to keep my wife from her own gift."

Santino rips his shirt off and I place my palms on his chest straight away. I run my fingers around the scar on his shoulder first, then across the scar below his ribs that's still bright red.

Santino closes his eyes and swallows hard. He's been reluctant to let me touch his scars since they healed.

"You're not any less devilishly handsome or roguishly sexy to me. In fact, I like my gift even more than the first time I unwrapped it. These scars are a part of our story. I see a battle-scarred warrior who fought to stay alive and come back to me. I love them, Santino."

He grips my chin, hypnotizing me with the depth of his gaze, drowning me in their dark chocolate. "I love you, Mia."

"I love you, too."

Santino's lips crush against mine just as I get the last word out, and the intensity of the moment only adds fuel to the already raging fire between us.

The best thing Santino ever did was be crazy enough to make me marry him.

ACKNOWLEDGMENTS

Thank you to all of you fabulous readers for keeping me writing and keeping the Carfano men and women on the forefront of my brain!

And a major thank you to all the espresso I drowned my body in to finish this book! You're the MVP of my marathon writing sessions!

ABOUT THE AUTHOR

Rebecca is a dreamer through and through with permanent wanderlust. She has an endless list of places to go and see, hoping to one day experience the world and all it has to offer.

She's a Jersey girl who dreams of living in a place with freezing cold winters and lots of snow! When she's not writing, you can find her planning her next road trip and drinking copious amounts of coffee (preferably iced!).

newsletter, blog, shop, and links to all social media:
www.rebeccagannon.com

Follow me on Instagram to stay up-to-date on new releases, sales, teasers, giveaways, and so much more!
@rebeccagannon_author

Printed in Great Britain
by Amazon